"I'm a doctor," she said. "Taking care of people is my job."

An anchor of guilt settled in his gut. Her heart was in the right place. "Okay then, Dr. Campbell. Please, doctor me up."

A hint of a smile curved on her rose-tinted lips. He tried not to notice, but she was even more beautiful when she smiled. Noticing Lexie's beauty felt like a small betrayal to Kristin. His late wife was dead, though, and admiring another woman was harmless.

"I'll be right back." Lexie jogged downstairs and was standing back in his living room with a medium-sized black bag a moment later. He dutifully laid his forearm down for her to inspect.

Her forehead creased as she leaned forward. "You need to take better care of yourself."

He'd heard that before. "Is that your medical opinion?" he asked. She smiled again, and he felt like he'd just won a contest. When he wasn't resisting her, he found himself being pulled toward her.

Annie Hemby lives on the east coast with her husband, three children and a rambunctious rescue dog named Carter. Annie loves to start her days with prayer and a good cup of coffee and end them praying with her children at bedtime. When she's not running after her kids and Carter, Annie combines her love for God and writing to pen heartwarming inspirational romance. You can contact Annie by email at anniehemby@gmail.com.

Books by Annie Hemby

Love Inspired

Healing His Widowed Heart

Healing His Widowed Heart

Annie Hemby

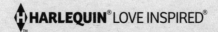

LOVE INSPIRED BOOKS

Recycling programs
for this product may
not exist in your area.

ISBN-13: 978-0-373-62301-3

Healing His Widowed Heart

www.Harlequin.com

Printed in U.S.A.

"For I know the plans I have for you," declares
the Lord, "plans to prosper you and not to harm
you, plans to give you hope and a future."
—*Jeremiah* 29:11

Trust in the Lord with all your heart
and lean not on your own understanding.
—*Proverbs* 3:5

This book is dedicated to my parents.
To Mom for your support and encouragement
in all my endeavors. To Dad for teaching me
that no goal was beyond reach. I love you.

Acknowledgments

First, I want to give thanks to God for giving
me a passion for writing and for this amazing
opportunity to work with Love Inspired.

A big thanks also goes to my family and friends
who are a bottomless well of support and
encouragement. To Rachel for making
my writing better and my stories stronger.

To my tireless literary agent, Sarah Younger—
thank you for your guidance and expertise.

I would also like to thank the Love Inspired
team, especially my editor, Shana Asaro,
for holding the From Blurb to Book pitch
contest and taking a chance on
Healing His Widowed Heart.
I have enjoyed every moment
of this new and exciting experience!

Chapter One

Smoke burned the back of Lexie Campbell's throat as she took a breath and kept walking, staying clear of the officers guarding her evacuated neighborhood. She only needed to get inside her home for five minutes—just long enough to grab the dress.

Heart pounding, she edged along the woods behind a row of houses. From the news, she knew the wildfire was still a mile away. She'd be completely safe to go to the house she'd rented for the summer and retrieve the only thing of importance she'd brought with her. She'd always dreamed of wearing her grandmother's dress on her wedding day—a day that was supposed to be two weeks from now.

Change in plans.

Tree limbs crunched loudly beneath her leather boots as she broke into a run. Bringing the dress here had been foolish. She'd come to Carolina Shores, North Carolina to take her mind off her problems and focus on helping others. That was her grandmother's remedy for a broken heart. Not the kind of medicine that Lexie practiced, but her grandma Jean had always known best. When Dr. Marcus had called to ask for help opening a free health care clinic here, Lexie had jumped at the chance. Looking at the black, smoke-filled sky now, she wondered if her decision had been rash. Unlike her ex-fiancé, though, she kept her commitments.

Seeing the house ahead, Lexie breathed a sigh of relief, which ended in a fit of coughing. She hurried toward the front porch and quickly unlocked the door. Inside, the air was stale, the smoke already seeping through the poorly insulated walls. She ran into the back bedroom and grabbed the dress from the closet. In the kitchen, she found a black garbage bag and stuffed the white-laced fabric inside. She wished she could throw herself in the bag right now. Surely no air was better than this.

Her head spun as she cinched the bag tightly.

Time to get out of here!

She hurried out the front door, making the mistake of sucking in another deep breath. Coughing again, she stumbled down the steps and started to cut across the lawn, heading in the direction of the neighborhood's front entrance. No reason to sneak around now. She'd left her car parked along the roadside. If she could just make it back, then she'd be fine. After arriving and unloading her belongings here late last week, she'd gone away for the weekend to visit a friend, taking a few changes of clothes and her toiletries with her, which were still in her car—a blessing in disguise. Little had she known she'd be returning to a neighborhood evacuation.

Lexie didn't bother glancing around to make sure she went unnoticed. No one was here. Everyone in Chesterfield Estates had evacuated. And with good reason, she thought now, feeling her world tilt and re-center like a ride at the amusement park.

A siren stopped her in her tracks. Looking up, Lexie saw a man with dark hair and a hard jawline leaning toward the passenger-side window of a white pickup truck. It was marked with the local fire department's logo.

"What are you doing out here?" he called. "Don't you know there's a mandatory evacuation in this neighborhood?"

Lexie erupted into a fit of coughing as she tried to explain. She wasn't a material girl, but the dress was sentimental to her. She couldn't risk letting it burn up in the forest fire.

Stumbling toward him, Lexie doubled over as she coughed. "I…was just…"

Just about to fall over if I don't get fresh air soon.

"Get in," he ordered.

Lexie straightened, still wheezing. "Am I under arrest?" she asked through painful speech.

His brows lowered over disapproving blue eyes. "I'm not a cop. If I were, then absolutely. Being here right now is against the law."

She approached his vehicle and pulled weakly on the door's handle. She'd gladly accept a ride into fresh air. If not for him, she wasn't sure she'd have made it out of the neighborhood and back to her car without collapsing. Clearly she'd misjudged the situation.

She tried to open the door, but her hands wouldn't work.

"Ma'am?" she heard him say, although his voice was fading quickly. She thought she heard his truck door open, and then two hands turned her around and firmly grasped the front of her shoulders. "Ma'am? Are you okay?" He leveled his eyes with hers, forcing her to look at him.

Her knees went weak and not because of his rugged good looks, which didn't go unnoticed even in her condition.

"Take a deep breath," he told her, his voice calm and in control.

Her vision grew dim. She clutched the fabric of his shirt in her hand, holding on to him so that she didn't fall. The garbage bag that she'd stuffed the dress into minutes earlier dropped to the ground below. "Don't let me die," she pleaded, feeling her legs buckle. Then she felt the weight of her body being swept up into the man's arms. He opened the passenger door of his truck and laid her inside as she struggled to hold on to consciousness, watching the colors around her blur like the view inside a kaleidoscope.

"You still there?" he asked, flipping the sirens on as he took the driver's seat.

The loud sound made her head throb. She tried to nod or say something intelligible. Instead her eyes closed, the world and the handsome stranger beside her fading away.

Mason Benfield had been hoping to find someone in the evacuated neighborhood, but it wasn't the woman lying across his passenger seat right now. On a tip, he'd driven through the neighborhood, looking for a teenage girl and suspected runaway. If the runaway was here, he needed to find her before she got hurt like the woman beside him.

He glanced over. The woman appeared to be in her mid-to-late twenties. And either she couldn't read, didn't watch the local news, or had a death wish.

He dialed 911 as he sped toward the neighborhood's front entrance a few blocks away. "I have an unconscious woman who suffered a possible asthma attack. We're at the entrance of Chesterfield Estates," he told the operator. He relayed a few more details, and then slowed the truck as he drove past the orange caution cones. He parked and got out, waving over one of the policemen enforcing the evacuation.

Mason wasn't up for giving the guy a lecture about making sure no one got past. If anyone, the woman in his passenger seat was the one who needed a harsh speaking-to. What she'd done had been senseless. They'd evacuated the neighborhood because it was dangerously close to the forest fire. They were trying to control the blaze, but one change in the wind and the flames could rage in this direction. The fire could engulf miles in a matter of hours. Walking inside the neighborhood on foot was a foolish thing to do.

As he scooped her body into his arms, she stirred, drawing his eyes down to her oval face. He didn't recognize her. Must be new to town, he thought, carrying her to a patch of grass near the road. He laid her gently on the ground, letting her legs drop first and then cradling her head until her soft auburn hair splayed out around her. He slid his fingers to the side of her neck and checked her vitals—good. Her complexion was rosy—and beautiful.

He breathed a sigh of relief.

"She okay?" the officer asked, walking up beside him.

Mason's jaw tightened. "Talk to your guys and make sure this doesn't happen again," he said, straining to hear any sign of help coming their way. "And keep a lookout for a teenage girl in this area. There's a suspected runaway that's been spotted around here."

The officer nodded. "Will do."

Mason couldn't stand the thought of a child finding themselves helpless in the dense smoke. Hopefully the girl had relocated. Hopefully, he thought, she'd gone home where she belonged. His late wife crossed his memory. Once a runaway, too, someone had helped her find her way. Because of that she'd founded the Teen Center, a cause close to her heart, and had helped a few dozen teens when she was alive.

Mason angled his head, listening as the sound of sirens grew in the distance. The woman on the ground stirred. Her eyelids flickered and then she reached for his hand. The feel of her skin on his was like silk. Reflexively, his fingers tightened around hers. He stared down at their interlocked fingers for a long moment, unable to break away. She was scared, that's all it was, which intensified his desire to keep her safe.

Don't let me die.

Her words back on the street had been too close for comfort. Pressing down the memories of his late wife, he nodded at the paramedics as they arrived.

"She breathed in a little too much smoke. Maybe an asthma attack," he said, as they carefully picked the woman up and laid her on a stretcher. His hand broke free from hers. Mason had the sudden urge to follow her inside the ambulance and ride along just to make sure she got there okay, to relieve her fears and tell her everything was going to be all right. He knew from experience, though, that sometimes things didn't turn out all right.

"My bag," she said in a barely audible voice.

Mason stepped closer as she was carried away on the stretcher. "What did you say?" he asked.

Her eyes opened just slightly. "My bag. I need that bag," she said, her eyes widening. Then she was lifted inside the small confines of the ambulance and the doors shut behind her.

What could possibly be so important that she would put it in a black garbage bag and risk her life to save it? Watching the ambulance scream into the distance, he climbed back into his truck to go find out. As he drove, he pushed back those haunting memories of the day his wife had died. His chest throbbed with the deep wound that the memory always reopened.

Everything is going to be okay, he'd told her. *The doctors will fix you right up.*

At the time he'd truly believed in what he was saying. He'd put his faith in the young doctors at Carolina Memorial, and his late wife had put her faith in his words.

Mason parked on the cul-de-sac and slipped on a mask this time because the air was thick. Just because he was a firefighter didn't mean he could gulp in smoke and not be affected. Somehow the woman had thought herself invincible. He grabbed the bag and carried it back to the truck. Inside, he ripped open the knot cinching the plastic, surprised when white lace fabric peeked through.

A wedding dress.

Which meant the woman on her way to the hospital was spoken for. Taken. Off the market. That knowledge stung a little, leaving him with something akin to disappointment, which didn't make sense. She was a stranger and he had no interest in dating or relationships, or ever getting married again. Shifting his truck back into gear, he headed out of the neighborhood with the bagged dress beside him. The smell of smoke was hard to kick. Foolish or not, he didn't want the bride-to-be to smell like a forest fire on her special day.

A short drive later, he pulled into a gravel driveway and parked.

"Mason." The woman he rented his garage apartment from turned from the stove as he walked into the adjoining ranch-style house. "What are you doing here at this hour?" she asked.

He set the garbage bag against the wall. "I thought I'd leave this with you for safe keeping if that's all right. I rescued someone from the fire earlier and—"

Clara Carlyle's hands flew to her mouth. "Are they okay?"

"Well, she wasn't exactly in the fire. She just got too close, and inhaled a lot of smoke. She'll be fine." That's what his head was telling him at least. His heart, on the other hand, was sick with worry. Ambulances and hospitals made him nervous. "Do you think you could check on her for me?" he asked. Clara checked on a lot of hospitalized people from church. It was something she enjoyed doing.

"Of course I will. I'm going to the hospital to visit Mr. Jacobs from the choir this afternoon."

Mason nodded. "Thank you."

"How are you doing?" she asked then, her brown eyes studying him intently.

A bunch of descriptions rattled off in his head. He was tired. Hungry. Anxious… Lonely. "I'm fine," he told her, grabbing an apple from her fruit basket on the counter and kissing her temple. "I have to get back to work. Then I'll be at the Teen Center tonight."

"You won't be home for dinner?" Clara asked with a frown.

"Maybe tomorrow night," he said. If the fire was contained.

"Be careful out there. I don't want to be visiting you in the hospital, too," she said.

Not a chance. "I will." He closed the door behind him and walked back to his truck.

Lexie awoke to the familiar sounds of a hospital. She was usually the one controlling the sounds. Now, for a reason she tried to remember, she was the patient lying in a stiff, narrow bed. There was an IV poking into her right arm.

Pieces of her morning started to reassemble in her memory. The rental home she was staying at had been evacuated while she was out of town. She'd gone back to get her—

Lexie sat up, her eyes suddenly wide as she scanned the room for her grandmother's wedding dress.

"You need to relax, dear." A short woman with white hair and a ready smile knocked as she entered the room, holding a large, leafy potted plant.

Lexie had never seen the woman before, so she guessed she was on her way to see another patient.

"I'm Clara Carlyle," the woman said, placing the plant on the nightstand beside her and pulling up a chair. "Mason sent me to check on you."

Lexie didn't know him, either. "Who?"

Clara smiled softly. "Your knight in shining armor. He rescued you when you passed out this morning. Don't you remember, dear?"

"Y-yes. I was going back to get—"

"Your dress. Yes, I know." The older woman looked sheepish. "I may have peeked inside the bag. Oh, it's a beautiful dress."

"You have my bag?" Lexie asked hopefully.

"At home. A hospital isn't the place for something like that. Neither is a fireman's truck. That's why Mason brought it to me. I'll take it to you after you're discharged. Where will you be staying?"

Lexie's mouth fell open. That was a very good question. The rental home had been cheap. It was run-down and needed renovations. Until she started her real job in the fall, she didn't exactly have the extra funds to rent one of the more livable, touristy places in town. She could always go back home to Raleigh, she thought, discounting that idea immediately. She'd promised Dr. Marcus she'd help him open and run the free health care clinic in Carolina Shores this summer. She would also be in charge of the clinic's outreach to the local teens in the community. "I'm not sure yet," she told the woman.

"You don't have any family in Carolina Shores?" Clara asked.

Lexie shook her head. "No." She'd needed a break from the concerned looks of her family and friends. They meant well, but seeing them only made her dwell on her canceled wedding and happily-ever-after.

There was another knock on her hospital room door. Lexie smiled for the first time since waking up at the sight of a short-statured man with an overgrown, scraggly beard. Dr. Marcus had taught a year of her medical school before returning to the field at Carolina Medical to practice medicine.

"Lexie! When I called and asked you to come to Carolina Medical, I meant to work alongside me, not to be my patient. Although it's always a pleasure to see you."

"Good to see you, too. And as soon as I'm discharged, I'll get right on that," Lexie promised. "I'm so excited about the work we're going to do together."

He smiled. "Me, too."

Clara stood to greet the doctor. "Hello, Dr. Marcus. How are you?"

He nodded and gave her a hug. "I'm well. Yourself?"

Clara patted his back and sat back down in the chair beside Lexie's bed. "I'm blessed. I didn't see you in church last Sunday." She lifted a brow.

Dr. Marcus shook his head. "I'm sorry I missed it. I hear the sermon was a good one, but duty called. I see you've met one of my favorite students from the time when I was a professor in Raleigh."

They both turned to Lexie. She'd passed her medical

boards last month. She was officially a doctor now, and couldn't wait to start practicing.

"I have," Clara told him, folding her hands in her lap. "Is she going to be okay?"

Dr. Marcus gave her a serious look. "You know I can't break patient confidentiality, Clara."

"So you keep telling me." Clara winked at Lexie. "He never tells me anything when I come to visit." Clara pretended to whisper, intending for Dr. Marcus to hear every word.

Lexie laughed. "Am I going to be okay?" she asked, turning to Dr. Marcus. "When can I trade in this hospital gown for my real clothes?" And start looking for a place to stay in Carolina Shores temporarily.

"Just as soon as you promise to stop running toward wildfires," he said, writing something on the clipboard in his hand.

"Oh, trust me, I won't be doing that again anytime soon," Lexie said. Heat moved through her cheeks.

"That's good, because part of being a good practitioner is setting a good example. Especially when it comes to the teens."

"Right." She felt conviction in her spirit. She hadn't started the job yet and Dr. Marcus was already mentoring her.

"And where will you be staying when you leave here?" he asked.

That seemed to be the question of the moment. Lexie knew that Dr. Marcus would offer her a place to stay if she told him she was now homeless, but she also knew he was a newlywed. He and his new wife were late to find love, and had only been married for a couple months. Lexie had attended the wedding here in Carolina Shores. It was the first time she'd visited the coastal town, and she'd wished she could stay a little longer at the time. Now she was here for the entire summer.

She opened her mouth to tell Dr. Marcus she wasn't sure, but Clara stopped her.

"She's my new houseguest, Dr. Marcus. A friend of yours is a friend of mine."

Lexie shook her head. "I couldn't let you do that. You don't even know me."

"You could and you should. Please," Clara said. "I never turn down an opportunity to bless someone in need. And you'll be helping Dr. Marcus with the new health care clinic. Our community really needs medical help for people without insurance. The least I can do is put you up in our guest room."

Dr. Marcus placed the clipboard under his arm. "It's settled, then. You're free to go, Lexie." He pointed a finger in her direction. "But be back in the clinic downstairs tomorrow morning and ready to start working the other side of the bed."

Lexie's head was spinning. She lived according to a plan, always had, and going home with a complete stranger was not part of it. But she didn't see any other option at the moment.

Clara stood and clasped her hands at her chest, looking excited. "Great. You get dressed and I'll wait outside for you in the hallway, dear. I'll call my husband and tell him the good news."

Reluctantly, Lexie nodded, forcing a smile. "Okay. Thank you," she said as Clara exited. Lexie stared at the closed door for a long moment, then started to put on her clothes. Another change in plans. This was becoming the theme of her summer. She'd been with Todd, her ex-fiancé, for so long that marrying him had seemed like the next logical step—even though she wasn't in love with him. That realization hurt. Then her plans had crumbled around her. So she'd planned out her summer here, and now her plans were falling apart again.

Okay, I can do this.

Clara Carlyle seemed like a nice enough lady, and since Dr. Marcus knew her, she wasn't exactly a total stranger. Lexie would spend her summer helping others at the health care clinic as planned, and then return home to the job that would be waiting for her in Raleigh. There would be no gold band on her finger at the end of the summer like she'd thought, but she was sure that was best. God's plans were better, Grandma Jean always said, and Lexie believed it. She'd been brokenhearted after Todd had called off the wedding, but she was trying to see the bright side. They'd gotten along fine, but maybe there was something, or someone, out there who was more than *fine* for her.

"Ready?" Clara asked as Lexie poked her head out of the hospital room.

Lexie nodded. "I left my car at Chesterfield Estates," she told Clara. "Along the side of the road."

Clara waved a hand. "My husband, Rick, works on cars for a living. He'll tow it back to our place. Don't worry, dear. He's excited about having you as a guest, too. It's the more the merrier in our home," Clara continued as they reached the elevators. "Our other houseguest lives in the spare room above the garage." She talked excitedly. "Did I hear Dr. Marcus say you'll be working with teens, too?" she asked.

Lexie nodded as they stepped inside the elevator and headed down to the hospital's first floor. "Yes. It's part of the health care clinic's outreach. I'll be helping teens learn about proper health care."

"Oh, that's marvelous. The two of you will get along just fine," Clara said.

Lexie was only barely listening. Her head was still a little foggy from her ordeal this morning. Something about another guest who lived in Clara and Rick's garage apartment. Lexie guessed she'd meet him when she got to her new summer home.

Mason hadn't been able to take his mind off the woman who'd broken through evacuation lines all afternoon. The fire covered a little over a thousand acres at this point. He needed to be focused on that instead. He also needed to find the runaway girl as soon as possible, before something happened to her. It eased his mind that Clara had promised to go visit the woman from this morning. Knowing Clara, she'd gone as soon as he'd left earlier and had probably taken a care package, too.

He wiped the sweat from his brow as he pulled the hose from the truck and handed it to one of the guys at the station. They were keeping the fire away from the roads while helicopters circled overhead dumping water where the trucks and firemen couldn't get.

His actions were on autopilot. There was usually a fire like this one every few years. Either someone had burned a trash pile too close to the woods on a windy day or lightning had struck dry land, such as it was in the current drought that Carolina Shores was suffering. No one usually got hurt. Of course, most people abided by the rules set forth for their own safety.

His thoughts drifted back to the redhead with eyes as verdant as this land once was. She'd risked her life for a wedding dress, which meant not only was she crazy for running toward a burning forest, but she was engaged. Somewhere out there was a man who loved her, who needed her to stay safe for him. She'd acted foolishly this morning and now she was lying in a hospital bed. The bride-to-be had been reckless with her health and her fiancé's heart—just another reason Mason planned on staying single. Loving someone meant the possibility of losing them, and he'd lost enough people he loved.

After spending another hour as close to the fire as he could safely get, he headed to his truck to grab a drink of water.

Fire Chief Henry Rodriguez stepped up beside him. "Your shift is over, Benfield."

Mason shook his head. "We don't keep to our regular shifts during something like this."

The chief raised a bushy eyebrow. "Let me rephrase that. You need a break."

Mason twisted the cap off his water bottle. Men with families needed breaks. No one was waiting for him at home—not anymore. Unless he counted Clara and Rick, who treated him like a son and always set an extra place at the dinner table on the chance that he'd make it in time.

The chief held up a hand. "It's not up for discussion. Get out of here."

Mason frowned. There was no arguing with his chief. He got inside his truck and drove to the Teen Center for a quick minute, then headed to the Carlyles' house. He was late for dinner, but at least he'd made it.

So had someone else, he noticed, seeing the unfamiliar gold sedan in the driveway. Clara was always caring for someone. It's what she did best. He wasn't a man who usually liked to be doted on, but Clara made it feel like he was doing her a favor when he let her.

Walking up the porch steps on the side of the house, he noticed a pair of woman's shoes. They were smaller than Clara's. More feminine. As Mason removed his own boots, something inside his gut rang out like a fire alarm detecting smoke. He suddenly had an uneasy feeling he knew exactly who Clara had invited for dinner tonight.

Mason shouldn't have been surprised. Helping people was what Clara did. That's how he'd come to live here. He entered the house as Clara set a steaming serving dish in the middle of the dining room's table.

"Oh, Mason! I thought you said you wouldn't make it tonight." She hurried over to hug him. "This is wonderful." She pulled away and gestured at the redhead standing shyly in the corner of the room. Mason recognized her from earlier in the morning, although she'd been unconscious at the time. "Look who else is joining us for dinner," Clara said.

Mason nodded. "I didn't expect to see you out of the hospital so soon," he said to the woman.

"Well, expect to see a whole lot more of Lexie. She'll be staying in the guest room here while her neighborhood is under evacuation," Clara told him. "And—" Clara clasped her hands in front of her chest excitedly "—Lexie is also going to be working with the teens in Carolina Shores! Isn't that wonderful?"

Mason stiffened. He was fiercely protective of the teens in this area, and he didn't know much about this woman, Lexie. The things he did know, however, led him to believe she was impulsive, foolish and not a person he intended to let the local teens have as a role model. Not on his watch.

Chapter Two

Lexie met the man's gaze. "Thank you for rescuing me this morning." She offered her hand to the dirt-smudged fireman in front of her. He shook it, and just that simple touch made her knees weaken. She'd always thought weak knees at the sight of a man were a myth. She was a medical professional and there was no good reason for knees to go weak just because…

Because when God designed this one, He'd tailored him with every trait she'd ever found attractive in the opposite sex.

She averted her gaze, hoping to steady her pulse.

"Nice to meet you under better circumstances," he said in a deep voice with just a hint of Southern drawl.

"I don't know what I would've done if you hadn't driven by."

"God put Mason in the right place at the right time." Clara turned to her husband, Rick, who had slipped into the room and was now seated quietly at the head of the table. "We can wait a few minutes, right?" She gestured to Mason. "A man deserves to be clean while he eats. Especially one who's worked so hard helping others today."

"Indeed." Rick nodded. "Of course we'll wait."

Clara made a shooing motion at Mason. "Go, go. When you come back we'll eat and get to know our new houseguest."

Mason frowned, glancing over at Lexie. She felt exactly the same way that he appeared to. Not that she didn't like Mason—he seemed nice enough—but she'd embarrassed herself with him this morning.

"Go on and clean up before the food gets cold," Clara told him. "We'll be waiting."

With a sideways glance at Lexie again, neither smiling nor frowning anymore, Mason disappeared down the hallway. Lexie stared after him. He was the tenant who lived here with Clara and Rick? The man she'd hoped to avoid for the rest of the summer?

She took a seat at the kitchen table and resisted any negative thinking. She'd kept her spirits up all day despite running toward wildfires and landing herself in the hospital. Living next door to a man she'd hoped to avoid the rest of the summer really wasn't that big of a deal.

A few minutes later, Mason reappeared, clean-faced and dressed in a T-shirt and pair of jeans. He sat at the table across from her and just the close proximity made her blood pressure rise. Her heart bounced around nervously in her chest. Lexie tried to focus on Clara and Rick instead of the man in front of her. Tried and failed.

"Let's pray." Clara turned to Rick. She extended her hand to him and to Mason on her other side. Mason took her hand and then reached for Lexie's.

Lexie swallowed, completing the chain by taking Rick's hand on her left and Mason's on her right.

Rick bowed his head. "Heavenly Father, thank You for the food You've provided for us," he said. "We know that You are our source. Thank You for these friends and family, old and new," he said, referring to Lexie. Then he prayed for the safety of the town and the firemen as the forest fire raged a few miles away. "Keep us all safe, Lord. You are our protector. In Jesus's almighty name we pray."

Everyone around the table said, "Amen."

Then Clara started to pass the serving bowls to the right.

"She does this every night," Mason said, serving himself several slices of honey-coated ham.

"And he rarely misses a dinner. Not unless there's an emergency. Or it's his night at the Teen Center." Clara smiled proudly at him, just as she probably would for her own sons if she had any. Lexie didn't see any pictures of children in the house, though, so she gathered that the older couple didn't. "You work at the Teen Center, too?" she asked.

"Oh, Mason runs the place, dear." Clara beamed.

"And I don't recall okaying any new volunteers lately," he said, lifting his gaze to meet hers.

Lexie swallowed. There was a hard tone to his voice that made her uneasy. "Dr. Marcus okayed it with you."

"You work with Dr. Marcus?" he asked.

Lexie got the distinct impression that Mason wasn't thrilled with her involvement. "Yes. I'm the new doctor who will be assisting him at the free health clinic."

She tried to smile. She was happy to be able to officially call herself a doctor. "I just passed my boards. Dr. Marcus was a professor of mine in medical school. He asked me to come to Carolina Shores and help him. He says there's a big need for medical care here."

"Oh, there is," Clara agreed, between bites.

"*Good* medical care," Mason said, his posture growing stonier by the second.

Was he implying that she wasn't good at what she did?

Lexie shifted uncomfortably. "Of course." She didn't want to take offense, but how could she not? Mason was suddenly glaring at her, like she'd said or done something wrong.

"Just because someone can't afford medical care doesn't mean they should get subpar attention from a new doctor, who's more concerned with wedding planning than medicine." He set his fork down. "And that goes for the teens in this town, too."

Okay, *now* she could get offended.

"I'm sorry, but I'm very focused on my role as a doctor." She'd wanted nothing more since she was six years old, lying in a hospital bed after her first asthma attack. "I graduated with honors from my class."

"Dr. Marcus wouldn't have asked Lexie to come to Carolina Shores otherwise, dear," Clara said, her brows bouncing nervously. Her fork was suspended in midair as she looked between them.

Mason wiped his mouth with his napkin, scooted his chair back from the table and stood. "I don't want to be rude, Clara, but I'm not very hungry anymore. I also need to head back to the fire early in the morning."

Clara and Rick exchanged a look.

"Oh, Mason, can't you just—"

Rick moved a hand to cover her forearm, stopping her from continuing. For the entire dinner so far, he'd been quiet except to pray. "Good night then, Mason. Be careful tomorrow," he said.

"I will."

They watched Mason walk away. Lexie forced herself to take a deep breath. She felt like she'd just failed an exam, except school was over and Mason Benfield's opinion of her shouldn't have mattered. But it did. The look of disapproval in his eyes just now stung. She'd been foolish to risk her life this morning, she understood that, but it didn't reflect on her skill as a doctor. Or it shouldn't have. Neither did the fact that she'd been planning a wedding for the past year.

"I'm sorry about that," Clara said, gaining Lexie's attention. "Mason gives all the young doctors a hard time. He hasn't exactly had the best experience with medical people."

So he was like 50 percent of the human population who didn't enjoy going to doctors' or dentists' offices, Lexie thought. That was no reason to be rude. She picked up her fork again and continued to eat, making conversation with her new Carolina Shores family. When the meal was over, Lexie retreated to the guest room down the hall, thankful for a soft place to rest her head, and for the fact that Mason had said he'd be leaving early in the morning. She wouldn't mind not seeing him before she started her own busy day tomorrow—her first at the new health care clinic. She'd also be going to see the teens as planned tomorrow afternoon, whether Mason Benfield approved of her involvement or not.

After a long day at work, Mason walked into the Teen Center the next evening and his whole mood shifted. He loved coming to this place that his late wife had founded. It had meant so much to her when she was alive, and over the years it had come to mean a lot to him, as well.

He high-fived one of the boys standing off to the side. "Hey, Albert. How are you?"

"Great, Mr. Mason," the boy said.

Mason kept walking, waving at the kids he passed, smiling and giving a high five every now and then. He stopped walking, however, when he saw the woman sitting at the end of the table. She was helping one of the girls with her homework. "What are you doing here?" he asked, a hard edge threading through his voice.

Lexie looked up, lifting her chin just slightly. "I told you I would be here. You and Dr. Marcus discussed this a few weeks back. You agreed to have someone from the new clinic come over to volunteer. That someone is me. I told Dr. Marcus I'd take care of this for him, so he could concentrate on other aspects of the business. I'm not going back on that commitment," she said.

Mason shoved his hands on his hips, speechless. There were a whole lot of things he wanted to say right now, but he didn't want to say them in front of the teens who were all staring at him. He wanted to tell Lexie that she needed to get up and get out. He didn't think that she had anything she could teach these kids that would be of benefit. Instead, Mason stared at her for just a moment longer and then continued walking to the office in the back. His good mood was gone. Now his neck ached from the tension pulling between his shoulder blades.

"Bad day?" his friend Dave asked, looking up from his desk as Mason stormed in.

"Not until now," Mason said.

Dave studied him. "Well, here's some good news. We have a new volunteer."

"Yeah, I know. And I don't want her here," Mason ground out.

Dave arched an eyebrow. "Why not? It's not every day we have someone willing to sacrifice their time. What's the problem?"

Mason crossed his arms in front of his chest. "The problem is… The problem is…" he said again, trying to think of a good reason why Lexie Campbell's presence was a problem. "Well, for one, she's careless. She's the woman who I rescued from the forest fire yesterday."

Dave nodded. "I know. She told me."

"And you don't think that's a problem?" Mason asked.

Dave shrugged a shoulder. "It's not like she's going to be telling the kids here that they should run into burning forests."

Mason shook his head. "I don't want her telling my teens anything. And I certainly don't want her giving them medical advice."

"I get it. This is because she's a doctor."

"A doctor that just graduated medical school," Mason told him. "She's barely got her degree and she'll be offering the people in this town, who you and I both care about, medical advice."

Dave considered this. "Well, she's been to medical school, and I haven't. So I'm assuming that she has better advice than I could give."

Mason pointed a finger. "You see? Even you would take her medical advice. That's why having her at the free health care clinic is dangerous. Just because she's a doctor, people will think her advice is golden. She's inexperienced. She can make mistakes that can hurt people. Mistakes that can kill people."

Dave's expression softened as he stared back at him.

Mason didn't want to see the look. Yes, he knew his past was influencing his opinion on this. He couldn't seem to help it, though. "Lexie said she's not leaving, so at least help me keep an eye on her," he finally said.

"Sure. But all she's doing is helping with the kids' homework."

"Good." Mason plopped himself down behind his own desk and ran a hand through his hair. He needed to collect his emotions before he went back out there.

Dave got up and headed to the door. "I promised Trevor we'd play ball. Catch you in a few?"

Mason nodded. "Sure." He just needed a couple minutes to himself.

After a few deep breaths and a quick prayer, Mason stood and walked to the glass window that looked out from the office onto the room of teenagers. He watched Lexie as she sat with one of the girls, Kim. Lexie threw her head back as she laughed at something that must have been funny to her. Kim cracked a smile for once, too. The teen girl rarely smiled.

Mason resisted the softening of his emotions. He didn't want to like Lexie. He didn't want her working here with the kids that meant so much to him. But Dave was right. The center did need all the help they could get. And truthfully, Lexie seemed like a nice woman. So, as long as she kept her medical advice to herself, Mason supposed that having her around was okay. It was just for the summer, he reminded himself. Then things would return to normal and the beautiful redhead would be gone.

Lexie was having a good time. Dr. Marcus had explained to her that the purpose of the outreach wasn't exactly to treat the teens here. Instead, it was to form a relationship with them. To give them somebody in the community that they could talk to. To make the medical professionals more approachable.

Lexie had worked with a lot of the youth in her hometown in Raleigh. She'd grown up doing community service and had always loved helping others. Over the past few years she'd gotten away from volunteering, however, due to her demanding schedule in medical school and planning for a wedding that never happened. This summer would be as good for Lexie as it would be the Carolina Shores community. She just hoped that Mason softened up a bit toward her. She didn't want to spend her summer tiptoeing around him.

She looked up at the office where he'd disappeared half an hour earlier. The door was still closed. She felt sorry that she was the reason he was blocked off from everyone. That hadn't been her intention.

The office door suddenly opened and her heart stopped. Mason appeared and started walking in her direction. *Here it comes,* she thought. Mason was going to try to get her to leave again. She braced herself. When she'd spoken to Dr. Marcus earlier in the day about Mason's stance on her being here, Dr. Marcus had encouraged her to come anyway. He'd described Mason as a big softy at heart. Mason's jaw was tight right now, though, the muscles bunched along his cheek—nothing soft about the man.

She swallowed and met his gaze as he stood behind her, overlooking the homework she was helping Kim with.

Kim looked up, as well. "Hey, Mr. Mason," she said, without so much as a smile. "Miss Lexie is helping me do algebra."

Mason's gaze moved from Kim to Lexie. "That's great," he said. "Every time I help her, she gets the questions wrong."

Unless Lexie was imagining it, Mason's mouth curved into the smallest of smiles. She took that as a good sign. "Math was always one of my favorite subjects," she told him.

He nodded again. "Then I guess we're fortunate to have you here."

Did this mean he wasn't going to escort her out of the building? That he'd had a change of heart? She offered up a smile in his direction, and then returned her focus to the algebra work sheets on the table. She pointed at the next problem. "Okay, let's try this one," she told Kim. From the corner of her eye she watched as Mason moved farther down the table and sat beside one of the teenage boys. Relief spread through her and hope blossomed. Maybe she wouldn't have to tiptoe around Mason Benfield all summer after all.

An hour later, Lexie drove back to the Carlyles' home to help with dinner as promised.

"Shall I set four place settings?" she asked, gathering the silverware.

Clara shook her head. "Just three. Mason called and said he wouldn't be coming tonight."

"Oh." Lexie swallowed and continued counting out forks and knives. "Is it because of me?"

Clara waved a hand. "No, it's because of him, dear. He just needs to work through his thoughts, that's all."

Lexie nodded, trying to understand. She didn't, though. She got along well with most of the people she met. His first impression of her hadn't been the greatest, but people deserved second chances. "I saw him at the Teen Center this afternoon," she told Clara.

"Oh?" Clara turned to look at her. "And will you be going back?" she asked, not so discretely asking the bigger question: How had Mason reacted to her presence?

"I'm planning on going a few nights a week after I leave the free health care clinic. I'll help with homework and play games with the kids." Despite Mason's initial attitude, excitement swirled around in her chest. "I'm really looking forward to it."

Clara nodded and lifted a serving plate to carry into the dining room. "That's good news. God will work things out. He always does."

Lexie followed behind Clara and sat with her hosts for

dinner. There was a void on the other side of the table. Even Lexie felt it. She ate quietly and helped Clara clean up after the meal. Then she retreated to the guest room, thoroughly exhausted from her first day volunteering at the health clinic and Teen Center.

She closed her eyes as soon as her head hit the pillow and thanked God for His grace today. Mason might not have been jumping up and down to see her this afternoon, but he'd allowed her to stay and, considering his reaction to her involvement with the teens the day before, that in itself was the equivalent of moving a mountain. Clara was right. God would work things out in the way He saw fit.

"Thank You, God," she whispered into the darkness, the prayer fading on her lips as she fell fast asleep.

The next day, Lexie woke refreshed. She grabbed a banana from the fruit basket on the Carlyles' kitchen counter and waved at Clara as she headed to her car to drive to the clinic.

"Bright and early," Dr. Marcus said, turning to wave at her. "Let's hope we see more patients today than yesterday. Not that I'm hoping for sick people. A few well-check visits would be welcome, though."

Lexie unloaded her belongings and slipped her arms into the sleeves of her white doctor's coat. She'd worn a pretend lab coat everywhere she went as a child, fostering this dream. Now she was finally a doctor.

She and Dr. Marcus stared at the clinic's unbudging front entrance, holding their breath until the door finally opened with the first patient of the day.

Mason's skin felt like it was melting as he worked the sidelines of the forest fire. Helicopters overhead dumped the water as fast as they could and the unquenched forest drank it. The loads were like spitting into a fireplace, though. None of it seemed to make a dent in putting out the blaze.

He stabbed his shovel into the ground, digging faster. All of the machines were busy making trenches where the fire was most threatening. If the winds changed, though—he'd seen it happen before—the fire would be heading this way, toward the schools.

And Lexie Campbell's rental home for the summer.

Guilt knotted inside his stomach. He regretted the way he'd treated her so far. He hadn't exactly been the most welcoming guy, even if he'd extended the smallest of olive branches to her at the center last night. He could deal with her assistance with algebra equations. Diagnoses and prescriptions, on the other hand, were entirely different. Lexie didn't have enough knowledge backing her medical advice. What if she made a wrong decision and someone got hurt in the process?

He shook the thoughts away and continued to work. A string of other firemen helped in the effort. A small trench would deter the fire long enough to get the machines over here if they needed to be. All of the firemen from surrounding communities were involved with the effort. Hopefully, within the week the blaze would be handled.

He stopped and wiped his forehead, resting against the shovel's handle. He'd been here well past his shift, but despite his chief's earlier encouragement, he couldn't leave. Besides, if he went home, the beautiful Lexie might be there.

Beautiful? Had he really just thought that? He preferred to think of her as an inexperienced doctor who needed to return to wherever she'd come from. Even though he had to admit having extra help at the center was nice.

Mason started digging again—harder and faster. Maybe the smoke was playing with his thinking.

A loud crack interrupted his thoughts.

"Heads up!" someone yelled through the trees.

His eyes immediately followed the familiar sound through the dense gray smoke hanging in the air. A tree was coming down. Maybe the fire had gotten to it. Maybe the vibration of the machinery on the ground had rattled an already fragile pine. His eyes darted toward the path the tree would most likely take in its fall. Everyone was safe. With a prayer on his lips, Mason began to run, too. The farther away he could get, the better.

A second later, the ground shook with impact.

Mason's heart raced and blood hammered his eardrums as he turned to inspect the damage. There was more danger here than just the fire. That was a lesson that the newer firemen hadn't learned yet. They would though, in time. That's why they worked as a team. He had everyone's back and everyone had his for the safety of all. In Mason's experience, that wasn't true with doctors. They had the backing of their own knowledge, and a new doctor had less knowledge than one with decades of experience. Maybe if Kristin had seen someone else at the emergency room after her accident, she'd still be alive.

Mason swallowed, pushing down the what-ifs. They didn't help. His wife was gone. She'd trusted him and the young doctor who'd taken care of her. Ultimately, it had been God's plan to take Kristin. Mason knew that in his head. His heart ached with her loss, though, and no matter how much counseling he'd done, he couldn't help feeling like he could've changed what had happened that day.

Mason walked toward the shovel he'd thrown down when he'd started to run. His cell phone rang in his pocket. He pulled it to his ear. "Hello."

"Hey, buddy," Dave said. "Trevor is on his way to see a doctor. One of the older kids is dropping him off."

Mason froze. "What happened?" he asked.

"A skateboarding accident. Don't worry, he's okay. Just a little scraped up. He's going to need a ride home, though."

Mason was already walking in the direction of his truck. Trevor was one of the teens at the Teen Center. He was a great kid with a big heart, who just needed a little extra adult influence in his life.

"I'm on my way to the hospital now," Mason said, picking up speed. He spotted his truck in the distance.

"I think he's going to that new health care clinic instead," Dave told him.

Acid rose up in Mason's throat. Trevor's mom worked two jobs, and they didn't have health insurance. No way was he going to let Trevor trade his fear of a big hospital bill for proper health care. Mason didn't want to see anyone do that, especially the teens. A lot of them came from low-income families. Some were smoking, abusing drugs, dealing with stuff that they were afraid to tell their parents about. They needed health care, of course, but not from inexperienced doctors like Lexie.

He climbed into his truck and cranked the engine. He needed to get to the clinic as soon as possible to make sure Trevor was treated by Dr. Marcus instead.

Chapter Three

A few patients had wandered into the free health care clinic this morning, but the pace had been slow. Dr. Marcus definitely could've handled this on his own, but Lexie was glad to be here. And hopefully, as word got out about the clinic, there'd be more patients.

When a teenage boy walked in the front door that afternoon, she turned to Dr. Marcus.

"Do you mind seeing him?" Dr. Marcus asked, pretending to be busy.

Lexie nodded thankfully and led the young boy back to her examining room.

"Where is your mother?" she asked as he climbed onto the table.

"At home. She told me to come here. It was just a skateboarding accident. Happens all the time," the kid said. Lexie recognized him from the Teen Center the other night. He was wearing an oversize button-down shirt and had a backward ball cap on his head. There was a grin on his childlike face despite the intermittent grimace that came when he moved his arm.

Lexie nodded, turning her focus to his wrist. She'd already palpated the bone and he'd nearly jumped off the table. His wrist wasn't broken, just sprained. A dark pool of purple blood resided just below the skin between his forearm and hand. She gently placed an ice pack over it.

"Ouch!" The boy shifted uncomfortably.

Lexie lifted her gaze to the rectangular bulge in his front pocket. "I'm more concerned about those cigarettes in your pocket. You're not even eighteen."

His mouth dropped slightly. "They're not mine. They're for my mom."

"I see." She twisted her mouth to one side thoughtfully, knowing a lie when she heard one. In the sterile room, she could smell the stale smoke clinging to his clothing. "Do you know the harmful effects that smoking can have on a body? You're young now and probably think you're invincible, but cigarettes are bad for your health," she warned.

The teenager stared at her, his eyes glazing over. He wasn't listening. He might as well have had earbuds blasting music in his ears like all the teens she'd seen around did lately.

"By the time you're my age, you'll be short of breath just going up a flight of stairs if you keep that up. You certainly won't be fit enough to ride your skateboard."

"They're for my mom," the teen said again, his gaze skittering to the wall behind her.

She frowned. "Well, in that case, you should tell your mother that I advise her to quit the habit and take care of herself, because she's worth taking care of. And so are you." Lexie pulled a pen out of her white lab coat and jotted down something on her prescription pad. She wasn't sure her patient was fully listening to her right now, and she wanted to make sure he followed her instructions. "Rest your wrist. Keep ice on it over the next few hours and take over-the-counter ibuprofen for the swelling. You should be fine by tomorrow, but if you're not I want to see you back here in my examining room."

The kid nodded. "Okay."

"And I'd give the skateboard a rest for the next few days. You don't want to fall on your arm again while it's healing."

The kid jumped down from the examining table. "Thanks, Doc." He took the paper and started to walk toward the door.

"And remember to tell your mother my advice about those cigarettes," she said, even though she was really advising him. "Quitting now will be easier than trying to quit later. Taking care of yourself is important."

Lexie opened the door for him and froze at the sight of Mason on the other side of it. "Mason. What are you doing here?"

His mouth was set in a deep frown just like last night. His gaze moved from her to Trevor. "I told you that you could call me anytime," he told the boy. "I would have taken you to the hospital."

"I just saw this doctor," Trevor said, pointing at Lexie. He held up the piece of paper she'd handed him, which outlined her care instructions. "See? Rest and ice. That's all I need."

"And stop smoking the cigarettes," Lexie added.

Mason's brow lifted. "Really?" He shook his head. "We'll talk later. Right now we're getting a second opinion on that wrist."

Lexie crossed her arms and took a deep breath, mentally counting to five before speaking. "I'm sure Dr. Marcus wouldn't mind doing that for you if that's what you need to feel better about my treatment of Trevor."

"I want the best for him."

Meaning that *she* was not the best.

She rolled her lips together and held her tongue, turning to Trevor. "Is that okay with you?"

The teen shrugged. "Mr. Mason is overprotective. He acts like my father sometimes."

She forced a smile, trying not to take Mason's behavior personally. "Nothing wrong with that. I'll just go see if Dr. Marcus can take a quick look." She gestured for him to take a seat in her examining room again. Mason followed behind him.

He was right. She was a new doctor, not skilled enough to complete brain surgery. But she'd known how to treat a sprain since she was in the Girl Scouts.

"Dr. Marcus?" she called, poking her head into her mentor's office.

He turned and offered a quick smile. "Everything okay?" he asked. "I saw Mason come in."

She nodded. "And he wants a second opinion on my patient." She blew out a breath. "Would you mind?"

Dr. Marcus stood and patted her shoulder. "I'm sure you did a great job, but if it eases Mason's mind, I'll take a look. He tends to hover over the kids from the Teen Center. That place means a lot to him."

She watched Dr. Marcus head toward the examining room that she'd just left, staying back and deciding to keep her distance right now because she didn't enjoy being doubted. And also because Mason made her nervous for more reasons than his scrutinizing gaze. He was handsome and she admired the fact that he wanted to look after the teens that he volunteered with. He was one of the good guys, even if he didn't trust that she was any good at the moment.

Mason glanced around as he walked out of the examining room with Trevor at his side. Lexie was nowhere to be seen, probably off treating another patient, he guessed. Good. He was a little embarrassed by the fact that Dr. Marcus had given Trevor the same diagnosis and medical advice that she had.

"No shooting hoops for you for at least a week. Your arm needs some R & R," Dr. Marcus said, following them out of the tiny room.

Trevor shrugged and mumbled an inaudible agreement.

"Trevor." Mason bumped him gently.

With a sigh, Trevor met Dr. Marcus's eyes. "Yes, sir," he said. "No shooting hoops for a week. Got it."

"And?" Mason urged.

Trevor grinned. "Thank you, Dr. Marcus. And that other doctor lady, too."

Dr. Marcus laughed. "You're very welcome, Trevor. Anytime."

Mason was as proud of his teaching the kids at the Teen Center as he was of putting out fires and helping kittens out of trees. "I'll take you home," he said, his gaze falling on the rectangular bulge in Trevor's front pocket. "And we'll talk on the way there."

"Hey, Mason," Dr. Marcus called as they started to leave. "The clinic's open house is next weekend. I was hoping you'd help."

"Help?" Mason turned back to look at the older doctor.

"Well, I know you're trying to raise money for the Teen Center. You could set up something outside to raise money for your group and to draw people in for us. It would help with the clinic's outreach efforts, as well."

Mason considered this. It wasn't the clinic that he had a problem with. Dr. Marcus was a great doctor and he'd told Mason just now in light conversation that other experienced doctors from Carolina Medical would be volunteering their time here, too, in the coming weeks. It was really just the inexperienced physicians that Mason didn't trust. Mason glanced around the room for Lexie, not seeing her. "I wanted to talk to you in more depth about those outreach efforts."

Dr. Marcus frowned. "Dr. Campbell is a fine doctor. And she's here in part to be mentored by me. She's not going to do anything to intentionally harm anyone."

Mason nodded. "She's been great with the teens this week." Not that he was happy about having one of them in her examining room. "If the wildfire is out by that point, I could spare some time for the open house. I'm sure a few of the other guys could, too."

Dr. Marcus clapped another hand along his back and gestured to one of the patients in the waiting room. "Great. I've got to get back to work. Good seeing you, Mason. Trevor. I'll see you Sunday at church."

Mason nodded. Then he led the boy to his truck and headed down the road, already knowing where Trevor lived. Mason had been to the run-down house a few miles away a couple times to fix a broken heater and a leak in the roof. Mason also knew that Trevor's mother wouldn't be home right now. She was working tonight, either at the gas station down the street or at her second job caring for one of the elderly members of the church they both attended. She was a well-intentioned mother who had little time to invest in her son, at least if she wanted to keep him fed and clothed. What time she did invest, however, appeared to be quality time.

"So, tell me what really happened." Mason glanced over at Trevor in the passenger seat of his truck.

"What're you talking about?" the teen asked.

"If you got that sprain on a skateboard, where's your skateboard?"

Trevor stiffened and his gaze averted out the passenger-side window.

That was what Mason thought. "We've talked about this. Fighting doesn't resolve things."

Trevor glanced back, but he didn't say anything, which told Mason he was on to something.

"And neither does smoking." Mason tipped his head at Trevor's front pocket.

"You sound like that woman doctor you treated so bad back there."

Mason stiffened now. "What are you talking about?"

"She was nice. Is it because she's a girl?" Trevor asked.

"I don't have a problem with girls being doctors. You know that. Besides, Dr. Campbell is a woman, not a girl."

"A pretty one. Is that why you don't like her? 'Cause she's pretty?" Trevor was smiling now. The kid was too smart. Somehow in the first two minutes of their "talk," he'd flipped the cards and was trying to shine the spotlight on Mason.

Mason frowned. "I know what you're doing, and it won't work. You're trying to make me forget about lecturing you on those cigarettes and fighting. You know better than that. How're you going to play pro basketball if you're carrying around an oxygen tank?"

Trevor crossed his arms at his chest, then winced at the pain in his bandaged wrist. He leaned forward, looking at the surroundings outside the window. "I thought you said you were taking me home. This isn't the way to my home."

"I called your mom on the way to the health care clinic. Told her you'd be going to the Teen Center with me tonight if you checked out all right. And then Mr. Dave would be taking you home afterward. She agreed."

From the corner of his eye, Mason could see Trevor

trying not to smile. He liked the Teen Center. "Fine. You got ice there? Both of those doctors said to rest and ice my arm. Means you shouldn't make me clean up when we're done, either."

Mason laughed. "Talk to Mr. Dave about that. I'm not staying. Not tonight." He had something else he needed to do. Something that was suddenly weighing on him like a ton of bricks. He wasn't a mean guy. The fact that Trevor had accused him of treating Lexie badly had convicted him just now. Lexie was just trying to help, which he admired about her—even if she was young and inexperienced, and he absolutely did not want her providing medical treatment for the people in his life.

Lexie finished writing in the last chart and released a long breath. They'd had a steady stream of people earlier in the morning, but the afternoon until closing had been slow. "I'm not sure you really needed me today," she said, turning to Dr. Marcus as he walked into the room.

He sat in a rolling chair beside her and laughed. "I couldn't have done today without you. I'm glad you're here. I hope you know that." His gaze narrowed.

Lexie shook her head as her mind trailed back to the incident with Trevor earlier in the afternoon. "I'm not sure everyone in town feels the same way."

Dr. Marcus frowned. "You're talking about Mason Benfield. Don't take that personally. It's not you. He…" Dr. Marcus's brows knit tightly together as he considered what to say. "He hasn't had the best of experiences with doctors."

"He didn't have a problem with you seeing Trevor."

Dr. Marcus smiled warmly. "You didn't learn this in school, but some people want a doctor to look a certain way. Whether it be male or female, old or young. There's at least one person in this town that thinks it's time for me to retire. She's accused me of practicing 'old medicine' on her. I just have to shrug it off and do the very best I can for every patient who comes to see me. Sometimes that means letting someone else treat them."

Lexie considered this. "You are still the very best teacher I've ever had."

"Thank you, Lexie. And you're the best student I've ever had, which is why I invited you to Carolina Shores to help me open this clinic. I'm sure there are a lot of opportunities in Raleigh, but this will be a great experience, I think."

Lexie nodded. "I think so, too."

Dr. Marcus stood, pulling off his white doctor's jacket and draping it on the back of the chair. "It's time for me to go home to my new bride."

The b-word sliced through her. She'd been so busy today that she hadn't even thought of her canceled wedding and happily ever after.

"You coming? Time for you to go home and get some rest, too." Dr. Marcus turned to her, oblivious to her sudden heartache. She wasn't sad because she regretted not marrying Todd, but because she regretted not having the wedding she'd put so much time and effort into. It was going to be a beautiful wedding, just like she'd always dreamed of, with white roses and bridesmaids' dressed in shades of pink.

Lexie rose to her feet and began to collect her belongings. Home. She wouldn't exactly call the Carlyles' place home, but Clara and Rick certainly did make her feel that way. Mason, on the other hand, did not.

She waved good-night to Dr. Marcus in the parking lot and got inside her car. As she drove, she listened to her voice mail. There was one from her best friend, who was currently preparing for a baby-moon with her husband.

"Last chance," Trisha said into the phone. "You can still decide to go to Hawaii by yourself instead of gifting the trip to me."

Lexie smiled at the message. She'd rather spend her summer days doing exactly what she'd done today. The next message was from her mother.

"Are you coming home yet?" her mother asked. "I'm worried about you being all alone in a strange place. And the news says there's a forest fire there. Are you okay? I love you."

Lexie turned her phone off and tossed it onto the seat beside her. She'd call her mother back after dinner. Pulling her car into the Carlyles' driveway, her heart sank as she noticed Mason's truck. She was hoping he'd be at the Teen Center tonight. She couldn't bear to see the disapproval or judgment in his eyes again today.

No, thank you.

In fact, maybe she wasn't feeling well anymore. Her stomach was no longer rumbling. Instead, it was tying itself into tiny knots. Clara would understand if she just went straight to bed. It'd been a long day at the new health care clinic, after all.

Getting out of the car, Lexie took a step toward the Carlyles' side entrance.

"Lexie?"

The voice was deep and even though they were still strangers to one another, she recognized it immediately. Turning, she faced Mason, who was standing in the dimly lit driveway. Her heart thudded painfully in her chest. She didn't want to fight. Like Dr. Marcus had said, some people had preferences for what their doctors looked like. She had to respect that. *Don't take it personally,* Dr. Marcus had told her. Except Mason's rejection since she'd arrived in Carolina Shores had felt very personal to her.

A soft word turns away wrath, she reminded herself. "Hi," she said softly. She tried to summon a smile as she looked up to meet his gaze. She didn't see judgment or disapproval there this time, which relieved her. "What's going on?"

He took a step closer, coming out of the shadows. He'd been waiting for her in the driveway. She could only imagine why. Trevor had come to see her just like any other patient. She couldn't apologize for treating him. She'd taken an oath to help people who were sick, hurt and troubled. Looking into Mason's eyes now, she wondered if he was one of those things, too.

Soft lines formed off the side of his eyes as he returned her smile. It was the first time she'd seen him smile so fully, and…it suited him.

"Can we talk?" he asked.

Chapter Four

Mason offered his friendliest smile, hoping Lexie would find it in her heart to hear what he had to say, which was that he was sorry. Not for feeling the way he felt, but for the way he'd made *her* feel. Judging by the look on her face, he'd made her feel awful.

"Please," he said. "It won't take but a minute." Her green eyes softened and she gave the smallest of nods.

He led her up the steps that ran up to his apartment above the garage. He didn't want the all-seeing-and-hearing Clara to be party to their conversation. Clara had a way of getting involved in areas of his personal life that he really wished she wouldn't. She was like family in that way, and he loved her like a parent. Unlocking his apartment door, Mason walked inside and turned to Lexie, who lingered in the doorway. "My bark is worse than my bite. I promise," he said.

She pulled her lower lip between her teeth and stepped inside, closing the door behind her. She didn't step any farther into the room however.

"I want to apologize." He shoved his hands into his pockets to keep from fidgeting. Very few things made him nervous anymore, but Lexie was making him anxious for a reason he couldn't quite explain. "I was a little demanding earlier. And insensitive. I was out of line," he rambled on, waiting for her to stop him. She didn't. Instead, she added to the list.

"Not to mention rude," she said, folding her arms in front of her.

"Yeah, that, too." He smiled despite himself.

"You think that Trevor needed a more experienced doctor," Lexie said.

"Yes." He watched as her posture stiffened. "That's how I feel." And he had good reason.

Lexie lifted her chin.

"No offense," he said. "I'm sure one day you'll be great."

"I'm good now. And I have Dr. Marcus's expertise to draw on if I need help." She hugged her body tighter. "You know what, I don't need your seal of approval to volunteer my time for a good cause."

"You do if you're going to provide medical attention for the people that I care about." He found his voice rising as memories of Kristin pushed to the forefront of his mind. He'd thought that he'd dealt with those issues. For the first year after Kristin's death he'd visited the church pastor for counseling every week. What had happened had been tragic. It was a rookie mistake by a first-year doctor, but nothing happened by mistake. God had a plan in everything that happened, even the things that hurt.

"Well, if that's all." Lexie turned on her heel and reached for the door knob.

"Wait." Without thinking, he reached out to stop her, grabbing her arm gently. "Don't leave mad." He'd brought her here to make amends, not to make things worse.

She whirled on him and opened her mouth, probably to argue, when her gaze caught on something. "What happened?" she asked, concern knitting itself in her brow line.

Mason looked down at his arm. "Oh. That. I got called to an illegal bonfire earlier. A bunch of high school kids had a fire too close to the woods. We already have one forest fire going out there. Carolina Shores doesn't need another. Anyway, one of the girls stumbled as I approached them and I had to catch her."

"You got burned," Lexie said.

"Not bad." He'd had worse. Burns and abrasions were part of the job description.

Lexie stepped closer. "It's bad enough. Did you put burn cream on it?" she asked.

"I'm a fireman. We firemen like our scars."

She didn't smile at his joke. "I have cream in my car's first aid kit. I can get it for you."

"Not necessary." He didn't want to bother her, and he had a first aid kit of his own. He was fully capable of applying ointment to his own wounds.

Hurt shone in Lexie's eyes as she looked up. She took his refusal personally, not that he blamed her after the way he'd treated her since she arrived. Even Trevor had noticed. "No offense," he said, holding up his hands. "I just don't want to bother you."

"It's not a bother. I'm a doctor," she said. "Taking care of people is my job."

An anchor of guilt settled in his gut. Her heart was in the right place. "Okay then, Dr. Campbell. Please, doctor me up."

A hint of a smile curved her rose-tinted lips. He tried not to notice, but she was even more beautiful when she smiled. Noticing Lexie's beauty felt like a small betrayal to Kristin. His late wife was dead, though, and admiring another woman was harmless. It wasn't like he intended to act on his feelings. He wasn't ready for romantic involvement yet, and maybe he never would be again. Besides, Lexie had risked her life for a wedding dress, which he assumed meant she was taken.

So why didn't she have a ring on her finger? he wondered now.

"I'll be right back." Lexie jogged downstairs and was standing back in his living room with a medium-size black bag a moment later. She gestured toward his kitchen table. "Let's sit over there."

He dutifully walked over and sat, laying his forearm down for her to inspect.

Her forehead creased as she leaned forward. "You need to take better care of yourself."

He'd heard that before. It was one of Clara's favorite things to say. "Is that your medical opinion?" he asked. She smiled again, and he felt like he'd just won a contest.

"Yes, it is." Her cheeks blushed a deeper rose color. "Not that my opinion matters to you."

"It matters. I just..." He wouldn't explain himself to Lexie. He didn't talk about Kristin to anyone anymore. After hours of counseling, he was done talking about it. "I'm sorry," he said again, flinching as she swiped a small square of gauze across his burn.

"Big baby." She grinned as she glanced up and met his eyes.

Those would be fighting words at the fire station. She was teasing him, though, and that felt like a step in the right direction.

"There." She applied a bandage and pulled away. "All better."

"Send me a bill," he said, joking with her. When he wasn't resisting her, he found himself being pulled toward her. He stood from the table. "Shall we?"

"Shall we what?" she asked, her mouth dropping open as if he'd taken her by surprise.

"Go to dinner."

Her bright smile fell like a shooting star, falling away into nothingness. "Dinner?" she repeated, looking at him like her new professional opinion might be that he was crazy. "You want me to go to dinner with you?" she asked.

And if Mason wasn't mistaken, she looked slightly horrified at the proposal.

Lexie took a tiny step backward, suddenly ready to bolt out of the room. She'd come up to have a private conversation with Mason, but he must've gotten the wrong idea. She was fresh out of a relationship—granted, it was one that had been over for a very long time. She wasn't looking for anything more right now, though, and Mason needed to know that.

"Um. I'm not ready to go out with other…" Her words floundered on her lips. Would it be so bad going on a date with Mason? Things had fizzled between her and Todd a long time ago, starting last summer when she'd barely seen him. She'd been busy with her studies and he'd been busy with his social life. Their goals were no longer the same. The things they'd once enjoyed doing together were no longer enjoyable as a couple.

In retrospect, she'd done all the wedding planning with very little input from him. She and Todd had become a business, checking in with one another about menial things. The foundation that a relationship was built on was unsteady. There was no trust between them as Todd spent time with other females. They didn't go to church together or study God's word in each other's company. Any feeling between them, especially love, was gone.

"I, uh…" Her gaze fluttered up to meet Mason's as she reconsidered.

"You think I'm asking you to dinner?" Mason asked, shaking his head. "I'm sorry. I just meant dinner downstairs. With Clara and Rick. They're probably waiting for us."

The blood pooling to her cheeks made her dizzy. "Right. Of course. I'm not ready to eat yet." She took another small step backward, needing to get out of this room before her embarrassment swallowed her up.

"Well, you'd better find your appetite because Clara won't take no for an answer if you're home. Everyone eats together." He was looking at her strangely. "Are you all right?" he asked. "I hope you didn't think I was coming on to you. I know you have someone else waiting to see you in that wedding dress of yours."

Lexie swallowed. Clara must not have told him that her plans had been canceled. "*Had* someone else," she said. "I don't anymore. We called the wedding off."

Mason nodded slowly, seeming to take this information in. "I'm really sorry to hear that."

Lexie shrugged, trying to act like it was no big deal. It was, though. Not marrying Todd was life changing. The perfect plans she'd made were gone. "I know you weren't coming on to me. Of course you weren't." She emitted a nervous laugh. Why would Mason be coming on to her? He didn't even like her half the time. She gestured behind her, taking a few more steps backward. "Anyway, I'll go wash up for dinner." She turned and started to leave.

"Thank you," he said as she left. "For doctoring me up."

Even if he doesn't want me to doctor anyone else in his life, she thought.

"You're welcome." The soft breeze was refreshing as

Lexie escaped out of Mason's side door and hurried down the steps. She'd gone from wanting his apology to considering a date that he wasn't even asking her on. He'd thought she was still engaged so there was no way he had been coming on to her. Maybe the oxygen deprivation when she'd passed out earlier in the week had muddled her thinking.

She entered Clara's house and slid off her shoes, leaving them beside the front entrance's rug.

"Dinner's almost ready, dear," Clara called as Lexie padded down the hall toward the guest room.

"Okay. I'll be right back." In the guest bathroom, Lexie quickly washed her hands and ran a comb through her red-colored hair. She couldn't help but think of Mason as she did. Eating a meal with him several nights a week would be a problem if she didn't get her emotions under wraps. While Clara and Rick were hospitable people, her neighborhood evacuation couldn't be lifted soon enough.

She headed back down the hall and into the kitchen. "What do you need me to do?" she asked.

Clara glanced back at her. "Oh, hello, dear. Can you grab the silverware and help set the table?" Her brow line pulled low over her gentle blue eyes.

"Sure." Lexie didn't budge. Instead, she continued to inspect Clara, whose face seemed to be frozen in a permanent wince. "What's wrong?" Lexie asked.

"Oh, just a little headache." Clara tried to offer her usual smile, but the movement made her wince harder, shutting her eyes momentarily and reaching a hand to rub her left temple.

"Did you take something for it?" Lexie asked.

"Yes. Don't worry about me. I'll be fine." Clara gestured toward the drawer again. "We'll need four sets of spoons and forks."

Nodding, Lexie opened the drawer and pulled out four spoons and forks. She carried them to the dining room table and began to place a set beside each plate.

"She's already putting you to work?" Mason asked as he entered the room.

Lexie willed herself to nod without looking up. Because when she looked at him her brain turned to mush and her heart started to patter against her will. She'd preferred it when she'd had ample cause to be angry with him. Now that he'd apologized and they'd come to somewhat of a truce, all that was left was attraction.

"You know what they say about idle hands," Clara chimed, coming through the swinging kitchen door and holding a steaming-hot casserole between her ovenmitted hands.

"Well, I'd work for food like this every night." Lexie scanned Clara's face again, looking for signs of pain.

"I could teach you." Clara set the dish at the center of the table beside two others.

"Really? I'd love that," Lexie said, meaning it. Cooking was a skill that everyone should have in her opinion. She'd never had time to learn, though. It seemed like her head had been in a book for most of her life. Now that she was on her own, skills like cooking were more appealing to her.

"I'd like that, too." Clara offered a small smile.

They all turned as Rick entered the room and removed his hat.

"All right. Everyone's here. Let's bless this food and eat." Clara pulled out her chair and everyone followed her lead.

Lexie tried not to look at Mason as she sat across from him. Embarrassment was still swimming through her. Why would she ever consider a date with a man who didn't want her to be a doctor to the people here in Carolina Shores? He didn't trust her professionally, and he'd made her feel sorry for her lack of experience on more than one occasion. Any dinner conversation they might have privately would only turn into an argument.

"Mason, honey, would you do the honors?" Clara asked.

He nodded and bowed his head. "Thank You for this meal, Lord. Please allow it to nourish our bodies. Thank You for this day and for bringing us all back together tonight. And thank You, Lord, for bringing our new houseguest, Lexie, here," he prayed.

Lexie stiffened at the mention of her name. He was thanking God that she was here with them. She'd thought he'd be begging God to send her away.

"You are so good, Father. Amen." Mason opened his eyes and looked up, meeting her gaze.

She offered a small smile, touched by his words. He smiled back and her heart started pattering again. It wasn't the most unpleasant feeling, she decided. Just one she hadn't experienced in a very long time. Not even with Todd.

Rick's voice summoned their attention. It was so seldom that Clara's husband added to the conversation that when he spoke the entire room went quiet. "I haven't heard much about the forest fire in the last twenty-four hours, Mason. Hopefully that's a good sign," Rick said, his voice carrying a low Southern drawl that Lexie had never noticed before.

Mason chewed quietly, glancing around the table. "It's contained, but it's still not safe to open up the neighborhoods closest to it. Especially for people with asthma." He cast an apologetic look in Lexie's direction.

Clara waved a hand. "Well, there's always a silver

lining somewhere. Lexie gets to stay a little longer. And cook with me," she added. Then winked and consequently winced at the same time.

Lexie reached for her glass of sweet tea. "That's right," she said, before coating her throat with the smooth, rich taste. Another silver lining was that next week was going to be hard for her, even if she had come to realize that calling off her wedding was for the best. She'd been planning her June wedding to Todd for over a year now. Next weekend was supposed to have been the happiest day of her life. Now it was going to be just an ordinary, uneventful day. Keeping busy and staying in good company was a blessing.

"How long do you think the neighborhoods will be closed?" Clara asked, holding a hand to her temple again. "Not that we're in a hurry to send you away, Lexie," she added.

"Probably another week," Mason said.

Lexie nodded. Just long enough to keep her distracted, and short enough that she could survive sharing space with the tall, dark and handsome fireman.

Mason finished up at the fire department the next day and headed to the Teen Center across town. The repetitive sound of a basketball hitting the pavement in the back of the building was a welcome distraction to his thoughts— the ones that had dominated his brain all day.

Lexie.

The brief misunderstanding between them had gotten his imagination working. She'd seemed interested when she'd thought he was asking her to dinner last night. She might have even said yes, which got him wondering how that would've worked. He didn't go on dates anymore. He had no idea how to relate to the opposite sex. He'd met

Kristin in junior high and they'd dated for what seemed like forever. Until she'd died.

"Hey, Mr. Mason!" someone called as he entered the building.

Mason turned to acknowledge Trevor, who was wearing gym shorts and an oversize T-shirt. "Hey, Trev. How's the wrist?"

Trevor shrugged, holding a basketball under one arm. "The pretty doctor woman was right. Rest and ice is all it needed. Now it's as good as new. She checked on it again earlier when she stopped by."

Mason lifted a brow. "Dr. Campbell was here?" he asked, looking around for evidence of Lexie.

Trevor nodded. "She just left."

"I see." Mason gestured to the basketball in Trevor's arms. "I thought you were supposed to take it easy for the next week."

Trevor dribbled with his good arm. "I don't have any pain. Wanna shoot some hoops?" he asked.

Mason hesitated, debating if the kid needed another lecture. Deciding to pick his battles—and this wasn't one of them—he nodded. "Sure. Let me go check in with Mr. Dave first. I'll be out in a few."

Trevor continued dribbling his ball between steps. "See you in a minute," he called behind him.

Mason kept walking toward one of the offices in the back. When he got to the doorway he stopped and waited for Dave to turn around. "We have a fund-raiser to plan. Dr. Marcus said we can set up at the free health care clinic for its open house on Saturday."

Dave grinned. "I'm shocked that you took him up on that offer. I thought you didn't like the idea of that place."

"I love the idea of free medical attention as long as it's quality care."

Dave nodded. "Still stuck on Lexie being there, huh? Well, a fund-raiser will help with the camping trip we have planned. I estimate we need about five hundred to a thousand dollars to make it happen. We still need tents and gear. Then there's the gas to get us to the campsite and enough food to feed a van full of teenagers."

Mason leaned against the doorway and crossed his arms. "I was thinking we could make the firehouse's famous Firehouse Chili for the fund-raiser."

"In the summer?" Dave's forehead wrinkled and his lips pulled down into a disapproving frown. Dave usually handled the business side of the Teen Center. The building was paid for. After Kristin died, Mason had used her life insurance to settle the bill. There were still utilities, though, and trips that the kids took regularly. The camping trip was a request from Trevor who, like several of the others, had never known his father. Fathers took kids on camping trips, Trevor had announced one stormy Friday night with all the kids at the Teen Center. He'd been exceptionally angry that week about things that were happening in his home life. That's when the guys that helped Mason run this place had decided that a camping trip was in order this summer.

"Yeah. Chili is for all seasons," Mason said. "The town loves it. We can charge three dollars a bowl. I thought we could bring one of the fire trucks out, too. Give the kids a little tour of it as they come in."

Dave was nodding thoughtfully at the idea now. "Okay. That might make us a few hundred. I have to work that night, but I can be there during the day."

"Me, too," Mason agreed. "I'll talk to some of the kids about coming out and helping."

"They'll love that," Dave agreed. "Maybe they could

even do a car wash or something in the empty lot next door."

"Great idea." Mason gestured behind him. "Trevor's waiting for me to play ball with him right now so I'm going to head out back."

Dave grinned. "Oh, I know. He's already asked me about a million times to go shoot hoops."

"So what's your excuse?" Mason asked.

"Punching numbers, as always. We have to pay bills around here. Then I'm heading out to go work the fire."

"How's the smoke?" Mason asked, thinking of Lexie again. There was no way she could return to her rental home until the air quality was better, even if her neighbors did. Her asthma attack had been scary. He didn't want to have to rescue her again.

"Still not the best. The forecast is calling for rain next week, though. That should help."

"Right." Mason straightened in the doorway. "I'll talk to you later, then."

He walked toward the building's back exit, pausing at the framed picture of Kristin on the wall. In the picture she was smiling, full of life and uncontained energy. That was one of the things he'd loved about her. She had no fear, unlike him, who was trained to know the danger in every situation. Lexie Campbell had no fear, either. She'd run toward a burning forest to save a dress that meant something to her. She'd agreed to stay with complete strangers in order to work for free over the summer. There were similarities between her and Kristin that he couldn't deny. Kristin never would've worked in health care, though. She'd paled at the sight of blood. The burn on his arm that Lexie had bandaged up for him last night would've made Kristin weak in the knees.

Mason glanced down at the white gauze secured to

his forearm, remembering the feel of Lexie's touch when she'd placed it there. Lexie had done a good job cleaning up his wound. She'd been gentle and efficient at the same time. And, if he were honest with himself, he'd gotten a little charge when he'd realized she wasn't engaged any longer. And at the suspicion that she would've said yes to having dinner with him.

Heat hit him as he stepped outside and was greeted by several cheers from the kids playing ball.

"About time, Mr. Mason," Trevor called, bouncing a basketball in his direction.

Mason caught it and started dribbling, forcing all other thoughts, including thoughts of Lexie, from his mind with each pound on the pavement.

Chapter Five

Lexie finished up her last chart and looked at the empty waiting room again. There was no way this place was going to survive without patients. She'd thought Dr. Marcus had said there was a strong need for health care in Carolina Shores. Looked like everyone was completely healthy at the moment. Hopefully the open house planned for this weekend would serve to get the word out. If nothing else, preventative medicine could be dispensed.

The front door to the clinic opened and Lexie smiled wide, ready to greet her next patient. Her smile fell like a stack of bricks, however, as she watched a man in a firefighter's uniform stroll in. His large stature made the room suddenly feel small, even though a minute ago the room had looked large and unoccupied.

"Hi," she said, sucking in a breath. He was just a man, she reminded herself, albeit one she found herself very attracted to. So much so that she'd considered going out to dinner with him last night during a brief misunderstanding. No big deal. Why wouldn't she want to go to dinner with him? He treated Clara like he would his own mother, battled forest fires, and had rescued her from an asthma attack last week. He was a regular hero. "What are you doing here?" she asked.

Mason headed toward the circular counter that she sat behind, just past the waiting room. "I'm here to see Dr. Marcus."

"Of course." Mason might have let her bandage up his arm last night, but he still didn't think she was a good enough doctor to treat him or the people he cared about. "He's in with a patient, but he'll be right out."

Mason was standing directly in front of her now. "I didn't come for medical treatment. I wanted to talk to him about the fund-raiser that the local firemen are doing here in the parking lot on Saturday."

"For the open house?" Lexie asked, wondering why she didn't know the fire station was coming. "What for?"

"The Teen Center." Mason leaned against the counter. "We're going on a camping trip in a couple weeks, assuming we raise enough money to buy the gear we need. We still have to get tents, sleeping bags, stuff like that."

"Sounds like a good cause."

"Yeah, well, a lot of these kids don't get to go camping with their families. They don't get a lot of things that other kids do, like a hot dinner or someone to help with their homework."

"It's a really great place for the kids to have. And the kids are so fortunate to have someone like you to care about things like giving them camping trips," Lexie said, adding to her list of things she admired about the man before her.

"See? I'm a nicer guy than you thought."

"I never thought you weren't nice." She sat back in her chair and looked at him, daring herself to meet his gaze to prove that last night's consideration of going on a date with him was just a temporary lapse in judgment.

"So, why teens?" she asked, wanting to fill the awkward silence.

Mason's expression subtly changed and, if she wasn't mistaken, sadness colored his blue eyes. She'd seen a lot of sadness in her life, especially working in the medical field. She could diagnose it with one look.

"What's wrong?" she asked. Most people volunteered because they were passionate about the cause. And, from her experience, people usually loved to be asked about their passion.

Mason shook his head, then ran a hand through his dark hair. "I, uh, guess you could say I inherited the cause. Someone close to me started up the Teen Center. She—"

The door to one of the examining rooms opened and Dr. Marcus exited along with his patient. Dr. Marcus's patients always looked happy when he was done with them. His enthusiasm was contagious. The same couldn't be said for Mason's enthusiasm toward the Teen Center. He'd told her that someone close to him had started the center. Since Mason now ran it, Lexie wondered if that meant the person who'd originally started the cause was no longer around.

"Hey, Mason," Dr. Marcus called. "What brings you here?"

"The fund-raiser. Got a minute?" Mason asked.

"For you, always." Dr. Marcus waved him inside a private office.

Lexie took her time finishing up her patient charts from the day, hoping to talk to Mason when he was finished with Dr. Marcus.

"Let me know if you need help at your fund-raiser on Saturday," she said ten minutes later as Mason walked out of the room where he'd been with Dr. Marcus.

Dr. Marcus waved as he walked past them. "Good night, guys. I have to run. Do you mind locking up for me, Lexie?"

She shook her head. "Not at all."

"Thank you." Dr. Marcus continued walking toward the exit. "I've got a date with my new wife and I don't want to keep her waiting."

Both Lexie and Mason laughed.

When Dr. Marcus was gone, Mason stepped toward Lexie. "I thought that you'd be too busy seeing patients on Saturday to help with our fund-raiser."

She shrugged a shoulder. "I hope so, but maybe I can slip away to help out if needed. What are you guys going to be doing?"

"Chili."

Lexie blinked. "In the summer?" she asked with a laugh.

"Why does everyone react that way? Chili is season-less. Trust me. The kids will get all the money for supplies that they need from this one fund-raiser. You watch."

Lexie grinned. "Well, I hope you're right. Sign me up for a bowl. I love a good bowl of chili. Summer or not."

"Can I sign you up for a tour of the fire truck, too?" he asked, lowering his voice and, if she wasn't mistaken, flirting with her. Or maybe that was her imagination, which had gotten her in trouble last night.

Instead of answering, she stood and began to clean up. The front door to the clinic swung open and a twenty-something man walked in.

"She's closed," Mason said.

Lexie laid a hand on his arm. "It's fine. He needs help and that's what I'm here for."

Mason turned to look at her, then offered a slight nod. "Okay. But I'm staying."

"You don't have to—" she started to argue.

Mason shook his head. "Dr. Marcus is gone. No way am I leaving you here all alone." He walked over and sat in one of the waiting room chairs. "I'm in no hurry to be anywhere." To prove his point, he grabbed a magazine from the pile beside him and started to read.

She should've felt offended, or at the very least annoyed. Instead, she smiled, calling the patient back. Mason was just looking out for her; he was being a friend, which was a step in the right direction from where they'd been only a couple days ago.

Mason glanced at his watch. It'd been a half hour since Lexie had gone into the room with her patient. He was beginning to wonder if he needed to go check on her when the door opened and Lexie walked out, wearing her white doctor's jacket and a smile that could heal all sorts of ailments. His usual work stress had fallen away as soon as he'd walked in and seen her face this afternoon.

"See you later, Chase," Lexie called after the guy, who looked considerably better than he had before he'd gone into the examining room with Dr. Lexie Campbell.

"Looks like you got along just fine without Dr. Marcus here."

She shrugged, stuffing her hands into her coat pockets. "That was an easy case."

"That you can't tell me about, right? Doctor-patient confidentiality and all," Mason said, finding himself smiling. It wasn't often that he caught himself feeling good after work. He loved his job, but it was demanding and stressful. The forest fire, while contained, was intense. There was still smoke and embers that reignited out of nowhere. One spark could ignite another situation like they'd had just a week ago.

"That's right. My lips are sealed." Lexie pretended to zip her lips with her fingers, which only served to draw his gaze to her oval face with high cheekbones and pale green eyes that were shining after her interactions with her patient.

Mason tossed a glance back to the front entrance. "I'll lock the doors while you do whatever you doctors do in patient charts."

Lexie laughed. "Sounds good. I'm almost done documenting. Then it's time to go home. I'm starving."

Mason grimaced.

"What's wrong?" she asked.

"Clara called while you were with your patient. I told her it didn't look like you or I were going to make it tonight. I didn't know how long you'd be."

Lexie's gaze moved to the clock on the wall above the front door. "Oh. I didn't realize how late it had gotten."

"That's called being in 'the zone.' It means you're doing what you were made to do." The front door clicked loudly as he turned the lock. He flipped the closed sign, turning it to face the public, and headed back toward Lexie. "How about I take you to dinner tonight?"

Her smile flatlined.

"You were going to say yes to me last night," he said, watching her cheeks darken.

"But you were talking about Clara's dinner table last night," she pointed out.

Mason nodded. "And you thought I was talking about going to a restaurant. It appeared that you were going to agree."

She didn't argue that fact, which pleased him.

"So agree to go to a restaurant with me tonight," he said. "Please."

Her head lowered, making a strand of hair fall into her

face as she sat behind the counter. "I don't know. It's just been a long day and I don't have a change of clothes."

He looked down at his fireman uniform. "Good point. I have a solution, though."

The skin between her brows pinched softly. "You do?"

"I do."

Their gaze locked. Yeah, he hadn't meant to say those two little words to a woman ever again. It'd been innocent enough, but it still brought his past slamming back into his present. It did something to Lexie, too, judging by the way she was looking at him.

"Okay. I'll just wait outside for you," he said, gesturing out the window. He needed a gulp of fresh air right about now. "Then I'll take you to dinner."

She nodded. "Okay."

When he got outside, he ran a hand over his hair. He had no idea what he was doing. He was acting without thinking, which wasn't like him at all. Not anymore.

His cell phone buzzed in his pocket. He ran his index finger over the screen to read a text from one of the guys who volunteered a couple nights a week at the Teen Center.

Jimmy says he saw the girl at the park.

Mason's blood surged.

Then the door to the clinic opened and Lexie walked out. "You ready?" she asked, smiling again.

The hot dog stand that he'd considered taking her to was located near the park. "Ready. Do you want to ride in my fire truck?"

Her mouth fell open. "Really?"

"Well, I need to return this thing to the firehouse and

get my real truck. Then I'll buy you a hot dog and a soda. How does that sound?"

"Like the perfect ending to my Tuesday."

"Mine, too." He led her to his truck in the parking lot. "Don't tell anyone that I'm giving out free rides, though."

Lexie grabbed the handle on the side of the truck and pulled herself up toward the passenger seat. "Mum's the word." When she was seated, she looked down at him. "On one condition."

"What's that?"

"You let me turn on the sirens."

He shook his head. "You're really just a big kid, huh?"

"Nothing wrong with that," she said.

Except she didn't look like a big kid from where he was standing. She looked more like a beautiful woman.

He didn't waste any time driving to the fire station and climbing into his pickup truck. "I need to do something before we eat," he said, as he and Lexie drove toward the park.

"What's that?"

"I got a tip about a teen girl hanging out at the local park. A couple of the guys and I think maybe she's making residence there."

"At the park?" Lexie asked, her voice rising an octave. "Like a runaway?"

Mason shrugged. "I hope not. But if she is, I want to find her and make sure she's all right. That's one of the whole reasons behind places like the Teen Center. To make sure kids have a place to go and someone to talk to." He looked over at Lexie. "Do you mind if we look for her first? She's been dodging me all summer and I don't want her to disappear before I get a chance to talk to her this time."

"Of course I don't mind. I insist, actually," Lexie said, which he'd known deep down she would.

"So your heart is bigger than your stomach, I see," he teased.

"So is yours."

He kept his gaze on the pavement ahead of him. Because if he looked at her, she'd be smiling. He could hear it in her voice. And there was something about her smile that made him want to keep making her smile. Her smile also made him wish he still believed in things like romantic love and happily-ever-afters.

Lexie fidgeted with her hands in her lap as Mason drove. Her hunger was replaced with adrenaline now. She didn't like the idea of a young girl, maybe a runaway, living in the park. That was no place for anyone, much less a child. Her mind swirled with all the health implications. The girl could be undernourished. She could have medical needs that were going untreated. That's one good reason Carolina Shores now had a free health care clinic.

"I'm sorry to drag you along. I should've let you go get your own dinner and done this on my own," Mason said.

"I don't mind. I want to help. That's why I'm in town. To help others." And to take her mind off weddings and honeymoons, marriage and happily ever afters.

Mason parked his truck and got out. Lexie met him at the driver's side while he checked his phone. "She could be anywhere. I guess we should just start walking."

Which was what Lexie had done all day. She'd walked back and forth from room to room at the clinic. It didn't matter. She'd keep going if it meant helping someone in need. They circled the park and navigated through the middle section, paying special attention to the benches and shady trees throughout. It was a hot summer. It only made sense that anyone who was outdoors for long would seek out the shadiest spot.

After forty-five minutes, Mason shook his head, running a quick hand through his dark hair. "She's not here."

"I'm sorry," Lexie said quietly. "We'll keep looking. We'll eventually run into her."

Mason nodded. "Yeah. I hope so." He looked at Lexie. "I promised you dinner, though, and I'm sure you're starving by now."

"It's hard to think about eating when someone out there is hungry."

Mason kept walking. "You've got the heart of a doctor, I'll give you that."

Lexie focused on the surrounding nature rather than on the handsome fireman beside her. "That's what my grandma Jean always said when I was growing up. I'd tell her I wanted to be a doctor and she'd say I was a smart girl, but heart mattered more than brains when it came to caring for the sick. Then she'd tell me that I had the biggest heart of anyone she knew."

"She sounds like a great woman."

"She's the best," Lexie agreed. "I really miss her." Lexie's throat suddenly felt tight. This was her first time feeling homesick since she'd left Raleigh.

They reached the hot dog vendor and Mason pulled out some dollar bills from his wallet.

"You don't have to—" she started to argue.

Mason placed a hand over hers as she started digging in her own purse draped over her shoulder. The touch made her shiver. "I dragged you all over this park after you worked hard all day. I'm buying. No arguments."

"Well, if you're sure." She removed her hand from her bag.

"I'm sure."

"In that case I'll just say thank you."

"You're welcome." He paid for two hot dogs and two sodas, then carried them to a nearby bench. She sat, taking her food, careful not to share any more unexpected brushes up against one another.

"So, tell me about yourself," Mason said, after a couple moments of quiet eating.

Lexie wiped her mouth with her napkin, hoping there wasn't any chili sauce around her lips. "There's not much to tell. I'm a doctor from Raleigh. I just graduated from medical school, as you already know."

"And you came straight here to work at a free health care clinic?" he asked.

He seemed genuinely interested in what he was asking rather than looking for a way to chip away at her credentials.

She nodded. "Just for the summer. Dr. Marcus is an awesome doctor. Any opportunity to learn from him is something I just couldn't pass on. Plus, I needed to get away from home for a little bit after...well, you know." Her voice trailed off as she stared down at the hot dog in her hands. When she looked back up, Mason's eyes had softened.

"Do you mind if I ask what happened?"

Lexie sucked in a breath. "My ex-fiancé, Todd, and I had been planning our wedding for the last year. We were actually supposed to be getting married this weekend."

"This weekend?" Mason repeated. "Wow."

Lexie shook her head. "Then Todd just realized that I wasn't the girl of his dreams."

"I'm sorry about that."

"Don't be. It's for the best."

"That's a pretty good attitude to have," he said.

Lexie blew out a breath in front of her. "Our relationship had momentum, kind of like a snowball rolling down a hill. It lacked love, though. And trust. And all the other things that a marriage is built on." She lifted her hot dog back to her mouth. "So I came here to help Dr. Marcus and learn as much as I possibly can." She felt the chili sauce smear around the corners of her mouth as she bit down.

"Which is good for us."

She slid her gaze toward him as she swallowed and wiped her mouth with a napkin again. "I thought you considered having me here a bad thing."

"I saw you with your patient this afternoon and with Trevor the other day. My teens are getting extra help on their homework and they think you're pretty wonderful. And despite starving, you came out here and helped me look for a runaway. I'm beginning to think you're a great asset to Carolina Shores. In fact, I know you're a great asset."

Her heart did a little dance inside her chest. "That means a lot coming from you. The truth is, you were right to doubt me, though. I've made a lot of mistakes in the short time I've been allowed to see patients."

"Everyone makes mistakes." Something flickered behind his eyes as he spoke. "Some mistakes are bigger than others."

"And some can't be taken back," she said, guessing that was his story. She just didn't know who in his life it related to.

"Right." Mason looked away. "I'm glad you have good doctors at the clinic to help you," he said. "Lean on them."

She swallowed, wishing she knew his story. "I will."

They finished their hot dogs and went back to his truck. Then Mason drove her to her car.

"I'm going to stop by the Teen Center before heading back to the Carlyles' house," he said, parking.

"Okay. Well, thanks for dinner and conversation." She turned to reach for her door handle, but he stopped her, laying his hand on her forearm gently.

"Wait," he said.

Looking back at him, her heart started bumping around again. "What?"

He pulled a napkin from his center console. "You have, uh, chili sauce on your mouth."

Heat ignited under her skin. She took the napkin from him and pulled it quickly to her lips.

"I didn't want you to be embarrassed if you had to stop somewhere."

She didn't think she could be more embarrassed than she was right now, having a chili face with an attractive fireman. "Is it gone?"

He smiled. "No."

She wiped again. Then he grabbed another napkin and reached up to help her. Sitting in the truck beside him was like aerobic exercise. Her heart couldn't beat any faster if she was running out of a burning building.

"There. Got it."

She pulled the truck's handle and started scooting in the opposite direction. "Great. Thank you. I'll, um, see you later."

"See you later."

She plopped behind the steering wheel of her own car a second later, cranked the engine and let the air conditioner blast onto her hot skin. One thing she was sure of—she was never eating a chili hot dog in the company of Mason again.

Chapter Six

Mason had spent the past hour patrolling the site of the forest fire. It was out and there'd been no sparks or cause to worry for over twenty-four hours. The air quality was still less than ideal, though, especially for an asthmatic like Lexie. She wouldn't be able to return to her rental home for at least another week. Not that he minded anymore. He was enjoying having her around, maybe a little too much.

"I'm heading back to the firehouse," Mason called to one of the guys standing nearby. Men were always needed at the station in case an emergency came up, like a car accident or house fire. And, cliché as it was, there was always that call about a kitten stuck up in a tree. He hoped that the rest of the afternoon would be calm, though. He might even wash one of the trucks to get it ready for the fund-raiser they were doing for the Teen Center on Saturday.

His mind returned to Lexie, just as it had all day. She was supposed to have been getting married this weekend. Instead, she'd be giving her time to help others. Most women, he suspected, would be holed up somewhere, crying their eyes out. And no one could blame them. A broken engagement was something to grieve. But Lexie was strong. Tough. He'd known that from the first moment he'd met her, breaking through an evacuated neighborhood to save a family heirloom.

"You're smiling," Dave said, walking toward him. "Why are you smiling?"

Mason realized he hadn't moved since he'd called out that he was returning to the firehouse. He wiped a hand over his face, scrubbing off the smile. It was evidence that he was thinking about her again. He needed to stop. There was no room in his life, or his heart, for anything romantic. "What's wrong with smiling?" he asked. "Maybe I'm happy to see the wildfire done with."

Dave looked suspicious, but nodded anyway. "Me, too, brother. Now we can return to our regularly scheduled summer. I heard you went looking for the runaway last night. Did you find her?"

"Nope." Mason slid the sunglasses on the top of his head back over his eyes. "Maybe she went home," he said, hoping that was true.

"Odd that she spends so much time outside the home. And those that have seen her say she looks dirty, hungry and kind of sad. I sure would like to see her clean, full and happy," Dave said.

"Me, too." Mason's stomach got that uneasy feeling as he thought of the girl braving life on her own. Carolina Shores was a relatively safe community, but there were still dangers.

Dave adjusted the hat on his head. "We'll find the girl. Just a matter of time."

"Right." Mason gestured behind him. "I'm going to go hold down the fort at the fire station."

"Good. It's about time you take it easy. You've been going nonstop over the last week."

Mason nodded. He'd have gone harder if his chief hadn't insisted on sending him home several nights during the fire. He was tired, though. A quiet afternoon at the fire station was just what the doctor ordered. "I'll talk to you tonight at the Teen Center."

Mason drove to the fire station and grabbed a sandwich from a tray in the kitchen. Clara had been by with lunch. She was like that, always taking care of everyone. Lexie had those same qualities. He ate and then handled a little outstanding paperwork that Dave hadn't gotten to yet.

"Want to help me wash a truck?" Mason asked one of the newest rookies in the group later. He tossed the rookie a towel.

He sat up straighter. "Yes, sir." The young fireman had likely been waiting for something to do all morning, while the men with more seniority handled all the emergency calls.

Together, they washed the truck, attending to every detail. When they were done, it shined like a polished apple. Mason didn't mind doing what no one else wanted to. He liked to keep his hands busy and his mind occupied. Today, keeping his thoughts centered on work was a needed distraction from thinking about the town's newest doctor.

His phone buzzed inside his pocket as he went to go get cleaned up. Lexie's name appeared on his caller ID. He hesitated. He'd given her his cell phone number in case she needed to contact him if something happened at Clara and Rick's house. "What's up?" he asked, pulling his cell phone to his ear.

"I think the girl is here," Lexie said in a whisper. "The runaway. Someone found her weak and disoriented in the park and brought her to the clinic. She's in my examining room right now."

Mason grabbed his truck keys and started running toward the parking lot. "Keep her there. I'm coming."

Lexie was taking her time with the girl currently seated on her examining table. "You were about to pass out at the park. Did you get too hot?" she asked.

The girl had shoulder-length blond hair that looked as if it hadn't been washed in over a week. Her fair skin was sunburned and freckled.

"Did you forget to eat?" Lexie asked.

The girl kept her gaze on the floor below her. She'd met Lexie's eyes once since coming inside the room. She had brown eyes with dark shadows underneath.

"I have food here. Crackers. Juice. Are you hungry?"

The girl picked at her fingernails, not answering any of Lexie's questions. Lexie had taken her blood pressure. It was normal. Her blood sugar was a little low, but not enough to keep her here or send her to the hospital. She'd told Lexie she was eighteen years old and that her name was Amber. Lexie doubted that was true. If there was nothing wrong, Lexie had no reason to detain her, except in her gut she knew there *was* something wrong. She just needed to keep the girl here until Mason arrived. Hopefully he would know what to say to get her to open up and trust them.

"Do you have a place to live?"

The girl looked up again, her brows pinching. "I'm fine. So if you're done with your examination, can I leave?"

"Amber," Lexie said, softening her voice. "Are you sure you're okay?"

Amber's dark eyes widened. "I said I'm fine."

Lexie held up a finger. "Wait here. At least let me give you some graham crackers and juice. You passed out and it's ninety degrees outside. I'll be right back." She offered up a silent prayer that Amber would listen. And that Mason would hurry up.

She opened the door and ran down to the kitchen at the back of the small building. She snatched a handful of individually wrapped crackers and a couple of juice bottles. Amber was exiting the room as she headed back. "Amber, wait!"

Amber turned.

"Here." Lexie held up the food. She grabbed a plastic bag from the counter in her room and dropped the items inside. She also pulled the clinic's business card from her pocket and dropped it into the bag. "You can call this number if you need anything." Not that the girl probably had a phone. "Or stop by and ask for Lexie. That's me."

Mason stepped up behind the girl.

Thank You, God. Thank You.

He reached over her and dropped a business card in the bag, too. "You can call that number, as well. That's mine."

Amber whirled around. "Who are you?"

"I'm Mason Benfield. I'm a firefighter here in town. I also run the Teen Center. The address is on the card. It's right down the street from the park." He lifted a brow.

"I'm eighteen," Amber said again.

"Doesn't matter. You can still come. We offer food and a place to get out of the heat. We play games, talk and hang out. You're welcome anytime."

Amber looked between them. "Do you have showers?" she asked, lowering her gaze to the floor.

Lexie turned to Mason.

"One," he said. "And a private bathroom. We also have clothes that people have donated. If you need something."

Amber grasped the bag tightly in her hand. "Maybe I'll stop in sometime," she said, not admitting anything.

Lexie wanted to keep her here. She wanted to wrap the girl, who didn't look eighteen, in her arms and force her to accept their help.

"I hope you do," Mason said.

Lexie watched him. If she had to guess he was resisting all the same things that she was.

He reached into his pocket and pulled out a twenty-dollar bill. "Take this."

Amber shook her head. "I don't need that."

"In case you need a cab home," he said, meeting her gaze and holding it. "Don't ever accept a ride from a stranger."

"Or food, right?" Amber tilted her head. "You two are strangers."

"I'm your doctor," Lexie reminded her. "Not a stranger anymore. And Mason saves people's lives for a living. He saved mine not too long ago. You can trust him."

Mason continued to hold out the twenty-dollar bill. "Please," he said. "Take this."

Amber pulled her lower lip between her teeth and took the money. "Thank you." Then she started walking toward the front entrance.

"There's no way she's eighteen. And I know she doesn't have anywhere to go, even though she told me she lived with her uncle," Lexie whispered, wringing her hands in front of her.

"I agree, but she does have a place to go now." He laid a comforting hand over Lexie's. "We just gave her one. She can come here or go to the Teen Center."

Lexie watched Amber disappear back onto the streets. "Right. And maybe she'll use that money you gave her to get a ride back to her real home."

Mason didn't look so sure. "Thanks for calling me."

"Thanks for coming." She blew out the breath she'd been holding ever since the girl had walked into the clinic. "I hope I didn't interrupt anything important."

"There's nothing more important than taking care of someone. That's where you and I are alike."

"Who'd have thought, right? You and I have things in common. We didn't even get along last week." Lexie laughed lightly, enjoying Mason's company. She was suddenly at ease in his presence. They hadn't saved the girl, but she felt good about what they had done.

"We just had a rough start, that's all. How much longer do you have before you get off shift?" he asked.

Lexie shrugged. "The clinic closes at six, but it's kind of dead in here."

"Go," Dr. Marcus said, walking up and overhearing. "You covered when I left early the other night. Now it's my turn to repay the favor. Let Mason show you around Carolina Shores."

"I wish I could. I'm actually heading over to the Teen Center tonight," Mason said, apologetically.

"Really?" Lexie removed her doctor's jacket and draped it over her forearm. "I was planning to go over and spend some time there, too. Do you mind if I come along?"

Mason angled his head. "Not at all. Especially if it gets me out of doing math homework. Plus, you haven't had the official tour of the facility yet."

Dr. Marcus placed a hand on both of their shoulders. "It's settled, then. Go, you two. Have fun."

Lexie stood from the small table where she'd been sitting for over an hour helping the kids do homework, and stretched her arms toward the ceiling. She'd always thought if she didn't become a doctor that she'd like to teach. She loved children of all ages. Being here was nice. She wondered if there was a similar place in Raleigh where she could volunteer after the summer was over.

"Hey, you." Mason snuck up on her and tapped her shoulder.

Whirling, Lexie faced him. "Hey, yourself."

"Sorry you got put to work as soon as we got here. I just need to make a quick phone call, but afterward, if you're still up to it, I'll show you around."

Lexie nodded. "Perfect. I told Britney that I'd watch her shoot a few hoops before I left anyway."

"You should," he said. "I'll just be five minutes."

Lexie waved him on. "Take your time. I'm not in a hurry."

She headed in the direction of the back door where she'd seen other kids going. There was a large bin of balls lining the wall just before the back exit. There was also a framed 8 x 10 photo of a young woman with dark hair and a pale complexion. She was pretty. Lexie read the name plate at the bottom of the frame: Kristin Benfield, Founder. The dates of her birth and death were listed below. Lexie's breath caught. The founder of the Teen Center shared Mason's last name, which meant they were related somehow. And the woman was deceased.

Lexie turned to look back toward the office that Mason had disappeared into. If she had to guess, Kristin Benfield was his sister.

Or possibly a late wife.

Lexie's stomach tightened. She forced her feet forward and went outside to watch Britney play ball. A few minutes later, Mason walked up beside her.

"There's probably no need for a tour. You've pretty much seen everything over the last week of coming here."

Lexie stood. "Show me anyway."

"All right. Follow me, Dr. Campbell."

He led her through the building, showing her where the kitchen was, the office, and the small game room where kids played air hockey and board games.

"Whoever started this place had a vision of how to keep kids off the street." She was fishing for knowledge, which was probably wrong. If she wanted to know who Kristin Benfield was she should just ask him.

"Yeah. She did," he said, turning to face her. "The founder was my wife."

Lexie's eyes immediately welled and she regretted saying anything. "I'm so sorry, Mason. I didn't mean to pry."

"It's okay. If you stay in Carolina Shores any length of time, you'd find out anyway. I'd rather you hear it from me. Kristin, my late wife, started this place. She had a passion for helping kids. I didn't think I did, too, but I was wrong. That, or she left her passion to me when she died. Kind of like an unexpected inheritance." He offered a sad smile.

Lexie swallowed. "She sounds like a great woman."

"She was." He sat on the table in the kitchen, clasping his hands in front of him.

"How did she…?" Lexie couldn't even utter the horrible words.

"Car accident," he said. "She hadn't even been too badly hurt. Or, at least, no one thought she had. The driver in the other car appeared to be in much worse shape. An ambulance took her to the emergency room anyway. The more experienced doctor took the other victim of the accident. He had several broken bones. A first-year resident took care of Kristin."

The puzzle that had been Mason Benfield was slowly coming together in Lexie's mind. "What happened?"

He looked at her. "She just had a headache. The doctor did a physical exam and let her go home. As I was driving her back to our apartment, I was telling her that when we got home I'd make her a hot cup of tea. Then I'd cook her dinner, anything she wanted. She'd been through an ordeal. I just wanted to make her feel better." He swallowed and looked down at his hands. "She laid her head against the window of the car as we drove. Just to close her eyes and rest, she said. When we parked in our driveway, I nudged her, but she wouldn't wake up. And that was it. She was gone." He blew out a breath and wiped the back of his hand underneath his nose.

"I'm sorry, Mason." Lexie reached out and squeezed his forearm. "It sounds like it was just a horrible accident."

Mason looked up. "I can't help thinking that if Kristin had gotten the more experienced doctor, she might have gotten a CT scan. They might have realized that Kristin's headache was a symptom of a bigger, deadlier problem." He shook his head.

"I believe that everything happens for a reason. God has a plan. At least that's what my grandmother always tells me."

"Clara says the same." Mason looked around the room. "So that's the story behind this place. Kristin left it behind and some of the guys at the fire station took it over with me. You have now had the official tour." He smiled, but it didn't touch the sadness that lingered in his eyes.

Lexie doubted the official tour usually included the story of his late wife's death. She felt touched that he'd included it for her. She didn't think Mason was a man who let people into his world easily, but for some reason he was slowly letting her in. "Thank you," she said, "for telling me about her." She swallowed past the impossible tightness in her throat.

"Thanks for listening," he said.

Chapter Seven

Mason adjusted the ball cap on his head to block the sun as it rose higher in the sky on Saturday morning. He had four Crock-Pots on the table in front of him. The chili ranged from mild to a mouth-scorching hot.

Glancing around, he looked for Lexie. It was the clinic's open house today. She'd be busy seeing patients right now. His chest tightened at the thought of a brand-new doctor caring for people in his community. He still didn't think she had the skill set or the backing of experience yet. He blew out a breath, hoping Dr. Marcus took the lead with those walking through the clinic's doors this morning. Nothing personal against Lexie. She was a nice woman and today would be difficult for her, he remembered. She was supposed to have been getting married today.

"Hey, Mason." Dave walked up wearing a T-shirt with the department's logo stamped across the chest. "What do you need me to do?"

Mason pointed across the lot at the fire truck. "You're on truck duty. Give the kids a tour and let them turn on the sirens every now and then."

Dave nodded. "You got it." He took off across the lot.

As he did, Mason's gaze caught on a girl standing by the side of the building. It was the same girl from the free health clinic a few days earlier. Despite insisting that she'd had a place to go, she looked like she could use a shower and a hot meal.

Mason started walking toward her. She stiffened when she saw him approaching.

"Hey, Amber," he said, putting on a friendly smile. "How are you?"

"I'm not about to pass out, if that's what you're asking," she said, referring to what had happened the other day.

He nodded. "That's good news. I thought if you weren't busy that you might want to help me with my fund-raiser for the Teen Center today."

Amber was about to shake her head.

"There's a free bowl of chili in it for you," he said, watching her eyes light up. "Two if you're hungry." Which he was pretty sure she was.

She shrugged. "I guess. What do I have to do?"

"Collect money. I'll serve the bowls." Mason thought that was best, considering Amber's lack of hygiene.

"I can do that," she said.

"Good. Follow me."

An hour later, after serving nearly seventy-five bowls, there was a lag in customers. Mason grabbed a bowl and poured some medium-strength chili inside, handing it to Amber. She'd refused to eat until she'd done her duty. "Here you go. As promised."

She smiled as she finally took it.

"Don't be shy about asking for more, either. You've earned it."

Amber nodded. "Thanks."

"Can I get a bowl of that, too?" a woman asked.

Mason knew who it was before he looked up. She had a serene voice that sounded like music to his ears. He imagined it was a calming voice for someone to hear when they were sick, too—even if she was a first-year doctor. "How hot do you like your chili?"

"Hot as it comes," Lexie said.

Mason glanced at Amber and grinned. "We've seen a few people start running for the fire hoses after a taste of our hottest variety. You sure about that?"

Lexie nodded resolutely. "Absolutely."

Mason gave another teasing glance at Amber. "Okayyy," he drawled, making Amber laugh. Lexie laughed, too, which did something to his heart.

"Thank you," she said as she took her bowl. "All that work this morning built up my appetite. It's nice to see you again, Amber."

Amber lifted a shoulder. "Thanks," the girl said quietly.

"I hope we'll see you at the Teen Center soon," Lexie added.

"Me, too. So," Mason said, summoning her attention. "The cook wants to see you take your first taste."

Lexie tilted her head, a playful glint lighting up her eyes. "You're hoping to see me run for the hoses. I'll have you know that I'm tougher than that, Mr. Fireman."

Mason nodded. She was tough. She had to be in order to put on such a happy face on what was supposed to have been the most important day of her life.

Lexie held up her spoon ceremoniously. "Here goes." She dipped it in the bowl of chili that he'd handed her and put it in her mouth. "Mmm." Her eyes closed momentarily.

He cocked a brow. "Good?" he asked.

"Oh, yeah," she agreed, nodding as her eyes opened

and began to water. "Haaaa," she breathed. "Whoo. That really is hot."

"Too hot?" he asked, sharing a look with Amber, who was nearly spilling over with laughter.

"I wouldn't say that." Lexie blew out another breath and laughed to herself while fanning her mouth. "Are you selling cold water, too?"

Mason chuckled. "Coming right up." He handed Lexie a cold bottle and tried to contain a grin, which was getting harder and harder to do when she was around.

"Maybe I'll do the mild version instead," she finally said.

He traded her a bowl of the milder chili. "How's it going in there?" He gestured toward the clinic. "Looks like you're getting a lot of business."

"We are." She sat on one of the metal fold-out chairs behind the table, talking as he continued to serve the intermittent customer. "We're doing what we call well visits today, checking blood pressure and blood sugar, weight and stuff like that. A lot of people don't get their annual physicals anymore, which is a big part of staying healthy."

Mason handed a bowl to a woman in front of him. "Be careful. It's hot," he warned. He could feel Lexie watching him, could almost hear what she was thinking.

"I bet you don't get physicals either, do you?" she asked when the customer had moved on.

He glanced over his shoulder. "I only go to the doctor when something is wrong." And not even then if he could help it.

Lexie shrugged. "I thought you liked to set good examples for the teens."

He looked at Amber to make sure she wasn't listening. "I do set good examples for the kids."

Lexie took another bite of her chili. "Maybe if they

saw you getting a physical, they'd get one, too. Growing teens need vitamins. They need to get checked out to make sure everything is developing properly. Just saying." Finishing off her chili, she stood. "That was delicious."

"Want another bowl?" he asked, happy to have a change in the conversation.

"No. I have to get back to work. Maybe I'll see you inside later."

She was still talking about him getting one of those well visits, which wouldn't be so bad. Dr. Marcus was working today. He trusted him. Two other doctors from the hospital with experience were also working. He trusted them, too.

And then there was Lexie. Checking blood pressure and weight was something that most anyone could do, so he guessed she was adequate for the job, as well. "Maybe so," he said, committing to nothing.

After lunch, Lexie returned to working the clinic. There was a steady stream of patients to be seen. Nothing too serious. The diagnoses ranged from the average cold to a sprained ankle. She was grateful for the distraction that the work provided her. She'd managed to avoid two calls from her mother, which she'd have to return later, and a call from her best friend, who would've served as her bridesmaid today. She'd also avoided a call from the man himself. Her ex. His message apologized for the millionth time. Todd hadn't meant to break her heart. He hadn't meant to send her running out of town. That's not what she was doing here, though. Coming to Carolina Shores was just her way of healing.

At six o'clock that evening, Lexie plopped down in her chair and sighed deeply. "Wow."

Dr. Marcus sighed in agreement from where he sat. "What a day. You really are a lifesaver to be here, working so hard for free."

"I'm honored that you asked me to help."

"We make a good team." He nodded. "Go. I'll lock up."

Lexie didn't argue. All she wanted to do right now was go home and kick her feet up. Or enjoy one of Clara's delicious home-cooked meals.

And not think about what could've been. Her engagement to Todd had never been right. What could've been would only have turned into a disaster, she reminded herself.

"Hey."

Lexie turned toward the deep voice behind her. "Hey yourself. I thought you guys left," she said, referring to the fire department.

"We did," Mason said. "But I came back."

"Did you forget something? Change your mind about getting a well visit checkup?" she asked hopefully. She realized now that he'd changed clothes. He was no longer dressed in his fireman attire. Now he was dressed in dark jeans and a pale yellow polo shirt that accented his eyes.

He shook his head, a small smile playing at the corners of his mouth. "No well visit checkup for me today. I did forget something, though."

"You did? What?" she asked.

"I forgot to ask you to dinner."

Lexie straightened. Was he asking her on a date? No, of course he wasn't. She'd made that assumption before and it'd cost her some dignity.

"I know today couldn't have been easy for you," he said gently. His eyes softened as he watched her.

"Oh. Right." *A pity date.* "I'm fine. Really. I'm not

even very hungry after all that chili I had at lunch." She attempted a smile, but it fell flat.

"Well, I'm hungry. And I don't like to eat alone. You'd be doing me a favor."

"But Clara cooks every night," she argued.

"I already told her that we wouldn't be there tonight."

Something about the word *we* made her heart ache a little. She was no longer a part of a "we." She and Todd hadn't been a "we" in a long time. Swallowing hard, she pushed back her emotions. She'd promised herself that today would be an ordinary day; that she wouldn't dwell on the past. Instead she'd looked to the future and focused on giving.

"Please," Mason said, stepping closer to her. He'd showered, too, she realized, smelling the clean scent of his aftershave. "Don't make me eat alone."

"Well, since you put it that way." She pulled her purse over her shoulder and waved at Dr. Marcus. "Just promise me we're not going out to have chili," she said as she walked beside him.

Mason offered a playful frown. "You said you liked my chili."

"Oh, I do." She nodded. "But I don't think I'll be wanting more for a while. Especially in the middle of summer."

Mason grinned. "Good point. So it's a yes? You'll come to dinner with me?"

"Yes." She walked beside him and allowed him to open the door for her. The air outside had cooled considerably since lunchtime. Now it felt refreshing. "I haven't really gotten to explore Carolina Shores since I've been here. Where are we going?"

"There's a little restaurant down at the end of the Carolina Pier. Best seafood around."

"Sounds perfect." She looked at her car in the parking lot and then at his truck.

"How about you ride with me and I'll take you back here when we're through?" Mason said. "That way we can talk on the way."

"Talk," she repeated, hugging her purse to her body. She was surprised she felt like talking to anyone right now. She hadn't called her mother back yet, or her best friend. Talking to Mason didn't fill her with dread at the moment, though. In fact, she was a little excited at the prospect of getting to know him better.

She climbed into the passenger seat of his truck and waited for him to get in on the driver's side. "So, did you get Amber to agree to come to the Teen Center?"

"I think she'll come. I told her there's food. What teen turns down free food?" He glanced over.

"Yeah. She seemed pretty hungry today. Poor girl. Did you get her to tell you any more about herself? Where she came from? If her name is really Amber?"

Mason returned his gaze to the road ahead of them. "Not yet. She doesn't fully trust me."

"She will. With time." Lexie resisted the urge to touch Mason's forearm on the armrest. Such a gesture seemed innocent enough, but she couldn't deny that Mason was attractive. Part of her urge to touch him was more than just to comfort him. She liked him—as a person. It was too soon to like him as anything more, and she wasn't staying in Carolina Shores. At the end of the summer, she'd return home to Raleigh. "Hopefully she'll show up at the Teen Center."

Mason glanced over. "I have to admit, it's been nice having you at the center. All of the other volunteers are a bunch of firemen."

"What's wrong with that?" she asked.

Mason shrugged. "Nothing, really. But the key word there is *men*. Some kids feel more comfortable around women. That's especially true for when we go on our upcoming camping trip. Do you camp?" he asked, parking in front of the pier.

Lexie shook her head. "No. I never have. My parents are more of the indoor type."

Mason was watching her, his smile carving out deep dimples in his tanned skin. There was new growth of hair on his jawline, giving him a five o'clock shadow. She was definitely attracted to him, which gave her a little hope. Maybe her heart wasn't as broken as people expected it to be. Maybe one day, a million years from now, she'd be ready to fall in love again. Or at least start dating again. "So what do you think?" he asked, his gaze locked on hers.

"About what?" She fidgeted with the strap of her purse. Had he asked her a question?

"Camping with us? I'm pretty sure we raised all the money necessary for equipment today, but we still need a female chaperone. Want to come along?"

Lexie froze. "Um. Well… I'm not sure."

Mason laughed and started to get out of the truck. "Well, then, I'll just have to convince you over dinner."

What had started as a mission to comfort a friend was quickly becoming a mission impossible not to forget that this wasn't a date. Not that he'd remember what a date felt like. He hadn't been on one of those since Kristin.

A thick lump tightened Mason's throat. "So, how are you?" he asked, shifting his focus to the woman in front of him.

She stabbed at a piece of fried shrimp. "Tired," she said with a laugh.

He didn't share in her laughter. "You know what I mean. How are you doing with today?"

"You mean the fact that I didn't get married today?" she asked, nodding.

"Yeah. That." He held her gaze as she rolled her fork between her fingers.

"I'm fine. Better than a jilted bride probably should be." She laughed nervously, but the emotion didn't touch her eyes. Most would be fooled by Lexie's smile. Not him.

"How long did you two date?" he asked.

"Too long." She looked up. "Three years. I was in medical school for all of that time, so really the time we spent together barely added up to a year. He was in school, too. We saw each other when we could, but our time together became less and less." Her mouth shifted to the side as she thought about her last relationship. "We drifted apart. I wasn't counting down the minutes to see him anymore, and honestly, I think we were both making excuses for why we couldn't see one another. We were friends, at best. Two people who are going to commit their lives to each other should feel more than that. Shouldn't they?"

The question caught Mason by surprise. He thought of his own marriage. Kristin had been his best friend, but it had been much more than that between them. He would've done anything for her. He loved her so much that a few hours separating them during the workday had seemed like too much most days. And when she'd died, the thought of never seeing her face again or hearing her laugh had been nearly unbearable. It would've been unbearable without the support of his friends and the pastor who counseled him after that. "Yeah. Marriage should be more than friendship," he agreed, clearing his throat.

He took a sip of his water. "So, why did you bring the dress with you?" he asked.

Her brow line dipped.

"The wedding dress you risked your life to save," he clarified, even though he was pretty sure she knew exactly what he was talking about. "Why did you go after it?"

"I told you. It was my grandmother's. And my mother's. I've dreamed of wearing it since I was a little girl. I guess I just wasn't ready for that dream to end." Suddenly her eyes watered and he regretted asking. "Silly, huh?"

"Not so much. Nothing wrong with sentimentality." Some would've called him sentimental once upon a time.

"Doesn't matter. I don't get to carry on that tradition. I'm going to focus on my career instead," she said resolutely, popping another piece of shrimp into her mouth and chewing.

"Your ex wasn't the right guy. Couldn't be," he said, wishing he could wrap her in a hug.

"Why do you say that?" she asked.

"Because he walked away."

Her eyes, still filled with tears, widened. "That's nice of you to say. But I'm not perfect."

"No one is. From what I've learned about you, though, I'd say you're pretty wonderful."

She looked at him again, a small smile lifting her pretty mouth.

They held each other's gaze for a long moment, and then Mason looked down at his plate. "So, what do you think of the food?" he asked, changing the subject.

"I think you're right," she said. "This is the best seafood I've tasted. Aside from the fish Clara cooked a few nights ago, of course."

"Of course. That's why I stay."

She took a sip of her sweet tea, studying him again. "My turn to ask you a question."

"Okay. Shoot." He set his fork down, bracing himself. He didn't like to talk much about himself, especially his past.

"What's the real reason you stay with Clara and Rick?"

He hesitated on his answer. "We go to the same church. After Kristin died they took care of me when I didn't care about anything. They're family. I'd do anything for them."

Lexie shook her head. "Look who's sentimental now."

"I lived in my old apartment for a while, but there were too many memories of Kristin there. Eating alone every night and watching TV was too depressing. Clara came to my house one day and demanded I come stay with them for the weekend. She's small, but she's persuasive."

Lexie smiled softly. "I've noticed."

"When I tried to leave after the weekend, she found reasons for me to stay. Her dishwasher broke and she needed me to fix it. Her fire alarms all needed new batteries. I'd do the tasks and she'd insist I stay for dinner afterward. Then she'd insist that my stomach was too full to drive back to my apartment and I should stay in their guest room."

"She's sneaky that way," Lexie added.

Mason nodded. "But I wasn't fooled. I knew what she was doing, and I appreciated it. The truth was I didn't want to leave. So I stayed."

"Funny how things work out," she said quietly.

In the dim lighting, it was impossible not to notice how beautiful she was. Her silk hair reflected the light and seemed to cast a glow around her. It was hard for him to tear his eyes away from her.

"For example," Lexie continued, unaware of his admiration of her, "I would've been preparing to leave for my honeymoon right now. Instead, I'm probably happier sitting in a small town and having dinner with a new friend."

She caught his gaze and they both seemed to stop breathing. It unsettled Mason because he remembered feeling this way one time before, with Kristin.

"Dessert?" the waitress asked, returning to their table.

Lexie started to shake her head, but Mason reached across the table and touched her hand. "I'll buy you a slice of chocolate cake if you say yes to the camping trip."

"Chocolate cake for camping?" she repeated on a laugh. "I think you've discovered my weakness, Mr. Benfield."

"Is that a yes then?" he asked.

"Yes to the chocolate cake," she told the waitress. Turning to him, she said, "And yes to camping. You've got yourself a deal."

Chapter Eight

Lexie sat behind the steering wheel for a long moment after Mason dropped her off. She wondered at the fluttering feelings that had swarmed and taken residence inside her chest. Today was supposed to have been her wedding day and here she was getting butterflies over another man.

A tall, dark and handsome firefighter who was equal parts tough and gentle. Serious and so funny that her ribs ached from all the laughing she'd done tonight at dinner.

Lexie blew out a breath and started to crank her engine when her phone buzzed beside her. She'd somehow avoided looking at it all evening with Mason. Now she stared at the screen telling her that she had five missed calls. Two from her mother and three from friends. The butterflies took a nosedive into her gut.

Pressing the redial button, she called her mother back. "Hey, Mom," she said when the familiar voice of home answered.

"Oh, Lexie. I've been trying to call you all evening. I wanted to make sure you were okay," her mother said immediately.

"I'm fine," Lexie told her. "I worked at the health care clinic all day and just had dinner with a friend."

"A friend in Carolina Shores?" her mother asked.

"Yep. And now I plan on returning home and going to sleep. A normal day." Lexie was impressed at her calm, level tone of voice. And at the fact that what she was telling her mother was one hundred percent true. Today had been a normal day, if not an extraordinary and wonderful day. Mason's face flashed across Lexie's mind. His company at dinner had been the perfect finishing touch.

Her mother was quiet for a moment. Lexie could almost hear her deciding whether or not she would believe her.

"It's okay, Mom. Really, I barely had time to think about my canceled wedding today. How are you and Dad?"

"Oh, honey. You're always thinking about everyone else. We're good. We just miss you," her mother said.

"I'll be home soon. I miss you all, too. I love you, Mom."

"I love you, too, sweetheart."

They talked for a minute more and then said their goodbyes. Lexie had owed her mother a call. She didn't owe anyone else one, though. Not tonight, at least. She pulled into the Carlyles' driveway and walked into the kitchen. It was only eight thirty, but the lights were off inside the house. Lexie wondered momentarily if everyone had gone to sleep. It wasn't unheard of to go to bed so early. Sometimes after a hard week, she'd fallen asleep much earlier than this on a Saturday night.

Lexie paused when she saw the shadowed outline of the woman sitting at the kitchen table.

"Clara. Why are you sitting here in the dark?" Moonlight shone through the window, highlighting Clara's face as she turned to Lexie.

She attempted to smile and then winced. "Another headache." She waved a dismissive hand. "I probably got too hot outside in the garden earlier. It's nothing."

Lexie put her purse down and stepped closer. "You should get checked out by a doctor."

"For a headache? No." Clara shook her head. "That's not necessary. Doctors have more important issues to deal with than checking on an old woman with a little headache."

"Well, I don't have anything better to do right now. I'm a doctor." Lexie laid a hand on her shoulder. "Let me go get my medical bag. I'll check your blood pressure."

Clara started to argue again.

"It'll only take a second." Lexie headed down the hall to the guest room and grabbed her supply bag. A moment later, she took a seat across from Clara and held up a blood pressure cuff. Slipping it onto Clara's upper arm, she pumped the cuff until it was tight around her biceps.

"All this trouble for nothing," Clara muttered, rubbing her forehead.

"It's not nothing. I care about you. You've taken good care of me since I've come to Carolina Shores." And of Mason, Lexie thought, feeling grateful for that fact, too. "Let me return the favor."

"Taking care of others is good for the soul, don't you agree?"

Lexie nodded. "I do." She frowned at the blood pressure reading. "Clara, your blood pressure is a little elevated." Which could be because of stress, but someone's BP shouldn't be so high when they were supposed to be relaxing and preparing for sleep. "High blood pressure can cause headaches."

"High blood pressure?" Clara repeated.

"When was the last time you got a physical?" Lexie asked.

"Oh." Clara laughed. "I don't go to a doctor regularly. I guess I should. Is high blood pressure serious?"

The last thing Lexie wanted to do was scare Clara. "Why don't you come see me on Monday morning at the health care clinic? I can give you a full workup and make sure there's no reason for concern."

Clara hesitated. "I don't know."

"Please." Lexie reached for Clara's hand. "It'll make me feel better."

"How do I say no to that? I don't want to worry you."

"Good." Lexie stood and yawned.

"Is the clinic open tomorrow?" Clara asked before Lexie could head down the hall.

"No, we're closed on Sundays, except for emergencies." Which Lexie had been called in for last weekend.

"Oh, good," Clara said, smiling even though her eyebrows were still tilted in pain. "Then you can come to church with us tomorrow."

"I'd like that," Lexie said, excitement sparking inside her. Dinner with a friend and a church to attend on Sunday. Carolina Shores wasn't where she'd grown up, but it was beginning to have the comforts of home.

Mason lay in bed, wide-awake. Insomnia wasn't an infrequent occurrence for him. He often lost sleep worrying about a victim that he'd helped at work or about the victims he failed to help. He lost sleep concerning himself with the kids that came to the Teen Center. He could only do so much in their time with him, but he knew the home life for most of them was less than ideal.

He did what he could, but he was sure that would never be enough. Not in his mind.

Give those worries to God is what Clara always told him when she noticed he'd been missing sleep. *He'll take them for you.*

Tonight, however, he wasn't losing sleep over any of those things. Instead, he was up staring at the ceiling and thinking about Lexie. He'd surprised himself with how much he'd enjoyed her company at dinner. It'd been a long time since he'd invited a single woman his age out for the sole purpose of getting to know one another. He was also surprised that he didn't feel guilty. The few times he'd looked or talked to a single woman since Kristin's passing, he'd been beside himself with guilt. Not tonight. Maybe that meant he was moving on. Pastor Diaz had told him that, while Mason didn't feel like the day would ever come, one day he might be interested in dating another woman. Maybe Pastor Diaz had been right. He'd been right about all the other advice he'd given during Mason's year of counseling.

With a deep sigh, Mason sat up and pulled the chain on his bedside lamp, flooding the area around his bed with light. He'd emailed a buddy at the police station to see if he could get some more photos of missing persons sent to him. He wanted to see if any of the photos matched Amber's likeness, even though she insisted she lived with her uncle. Mason didn't want to believe she was lying, but he knew for a fact that Amber needed help. Pulling his laptop toward him, Mason opened it and found an email from Detective Morris. In the email was a stream of recent missing persons in the state. Mason studied each one's picture carefully. None of them resembled Amber. Which meant that no one was missing her right now. The muscles along his jaw tightened. Amber was someone's daughter, sister, niece, friend. There had to be someone out there looking for her, somewhere.

Just one more reason to lose sleep tonight, he decided, wishing he knew what Amber's secret was. He wanted to help her. If Kristin were still alive, she'd know exactly how to reach the young lady with purple-and-blue shadows under her eyes. Kristin was good at elbowing her way into everyone's heart.

Lexie was good at that, too, Mason thought, lifting his gaze to look outside his window. He had a direct view of the Carlyles' house where Lexie was likely fast asleep by now. Despite his worry about Amber, a smile lifted on his mouth. Something was shifting inside him; he could feel it, and while it scared him more than any fire ever had, it also stirred excitement.

The next morning Mason walked downstairs and entered the Carlyles' house, breathing in the smell of freshly brewed coffee. He could use a cup this morning.

Clara turned and studied his face. "What's keeping you up these days? The forest fire is out."

Mason walked over and kissed her temple. "I'm looking forward to going to church this morning," he said, diverting her attention.

Clara took the bait. "We're in the middle of a series on Psalms. Make sure you bring your Bible."

"Of course I will." He lifted a mug from the cabinet and poured himself a healthy serving of coffee.

On autopilot, Clara retrieved the cream and sugar for him, setting it at the small table to the side.

"Where's everyone else?" Mason asked, referring to Rick and Lexie. It was Lexie he really wanted to know about, though. He couldn't help himself. He'd thought about her nonstop since dinner last night and now he couldn't wait to see her smiling face.

"She's still in her room, dear," Clara said knowingly. "Although she needs to get stirring if she's going to make it to church with us. Would you mind tapping on her door and making sure she's awake?"

Rick entered the kitchen and headed straight for the coffeepot. "And you might want to drive her to church this morning. Her front tire is looking a little low on air," he said, heading for the coffeepot, as well.

"Yes, sir." Mason nodded and set his mug of coffee down. He didn't need coffee to wake him up anymore. Just the thought of Lexie revived his energy. "I'll go check on her right now." He headed down the long hallway and paused in front of her bedroom door. He could hear movement inside. Good. He didn't want to startle her awake. He knocked softly. "Lexie? It's Mason."

After a few seconds her door cracked open. He was relieved to see that she was already dressed in a long, navy-colored dress with a yellow sunflower print.

"Hi," he said, holding her gaze momentarily. "Clara asked me to make sure you were still coming to church with us."

Lexie nodded. "Yes. I think maybe I'm overdue for a trip to church. I've been reading my Bible, but I haven't been to Sunday worship since I came here from Raleigh."

Mason smiled. "You'll like this one. Everyone's welcoming. About last night, I wanted to tell you that I had a good time with you."

"Me, too. Thanks for keeping me company," she said.

"Anytime." He held her gaze for a long beat. An electric current buzzed between them. "We better get going," he said. "Guess you'll have to ride with me."

"I have my own car."

Mason shook his head. "Rick said not to let you drive it. The tires are looking low. I'll put more air in them tonight." He silently thanked God for this fact. A little more time with the pretty houseguest was exactly what the doctor ordered.

"Oh. Okay," she said, walking beside him down the hall to the kitchen.

Mason served her a cup of coffee to go and then walked her out to his truck. "How'd you sleep last night?" he asked as he drove.

Lexie sipped from the thermos in her hand. "Like a baby." She turned to him. "You?"

"Not like a baby," he said. "But like I normally do, so no big deal." He could feel the weight of Lexie's stare.

"Sleep is important. If you're not sleeping, maybe you should—"

Mason looked over. "Get checked by a doctor," he said, completing her sentence for her. "I'm fine." He winked at her to show he wasn't upset by her advice, even though he'd never take it. Then he pulled into the church parking lot. The church was a classic brick sanctuary, one of three in the small town. Mason pulled up just as Clara and Rick were getting out of their own vehicle.

"She's got that look on her face," he said before opening his truck door.

Lexie chuckled. "What look?"

"The one that says she's up to something."

Clara headed toward his truck. Her red curls fell on her forehead as she smiled. There was something in her eyes as she waited for Mason to step out. "I forgot that I have duty this morning," Clara said, wincing.

"Duty?" he asked.

Lexie stepped up beside Mason.

"I volunteered to watch the three- and four-year-olds

today." Clara brought a hand to her head. "But I have a little headache this morning."

Mason stepped back as if Clara had thrown down a rattlesnake. "Oh. Clara, I manage the Teen Center. I don't do little kids."

"Could you two take nursery duty for me?" Clara asked, ignoring him and turning to Lexie.

Now Lexie drew back. "Both of us?" they chimed, turning to each other.

"Why both of us?" Mason asked. "You're only one person to replace."

"But I'm experienced. You can't do it alone," Clara told him.

"Then let Lexie do it."

Lexie turned to him. "Me? Why me?"

"You're a woman. Women like nursery duty," Mason said.

Lexie shook her head. "I've never even been to this church. People aren't going to just let me take care of their children."

"Exactly." Clara smiled, rubbing her head again. "Thank you both so much." She turned and started toward the front doors of the church without waiting for them to argue further. She did that a lot.

Lexie began walking ahead of him toward the church. She glared playfully at him over her shoulder. "Thanks a lot."

"What?" he asked, walking up beside her. "Little kids and I don't mesh. I'm too serious."

"No silly side of Mason Benfield?" she asked, lifting a brow.

He shook his head. "Nope."

"I doubt that's true, but I'm sure they'll love you.

They'll have to because it looks like we're all they have for the next hour and a half."

And that was the silver lining: more time with Lexie. Maybe taking care of little kids wouldn't be so bad, Mason considered, holding the door open for Lexie to pass through into the church.

Lexie laughed as she watched Mason, a big, strong fireman, playing with dolls. He had no difficulty winning over the three little princesses competing for his affection in the small pastel-colored church nursery.

"You're one of God's helpers," Hannah, a sweet little girl with honey tones, said, leaning against his knee.

He nodded. "I hope I am. You're one, too."

"Me?" She crinkled her nose adorably at him.

"You help the Big Guy when you help other people," Mason told her, feeling his heart strings tug a little bit harder. The girl was impossibly cute and she'd been clinging to him from the moment he walked into the room. He knew her father, a local marine who was currently deployed overseas.

"Oh." Hannah broke into a toothless grin.

"Why don't you go over and play with Sabrina and Jennie?" he asked. "Looks like they're having a tea party over there."

Hannah followed his gaze, considering this. Then she hugged him tight and ran over to play with the two other girls in the corner.

"You were wrong. You're fairly good with kids," Lexie commented. "You must have kids in your family."

He cocked a sideways grin. "Not really. I'm an only child. No nieces or nephews. A few of the firefighters I work with have kids, though. They invite me over now and then, and I end up babysitting." He looked at her. "What about you?"

Lexie shot a toy truck across the room, summoning a joyful squeal from one of the boys. "No nieces or nephews for me, either. But I have cousins and they have children. My best friend is actually pregnant right now." She felt her insides twist uncomfortably. It wasn't that she wasn't happy for Trisha, but she couldn't help but hear her own biological clock tick louder with the news. "Todd always said he didn't want children," she said, feeling emotional suddenly. She pressed the feelings down, studying her hands. She wasn't even sure why she'd volunteered that information.

"Well, it's not just the guy's decision. I've always thought that the woman should get a larger vote in that. She's the mother. She's got all those—" he fluttered his hands in the air "—chemicals and hormones toward children."

Lexie laughed, feeling slightly better. "The father has hormones, too, you know. I'm a doctor. I know these things."

Another little girl climbed into Mason's lap. "It's just different, I think. You and Tad…"

"Todd," she corrected, suspecting he knew good and well that he'd gotten her ex's name wrong.

"Yeah. Sounds like you two had very different plans for your lives."

Lexie nodded. She wondered about the warm feelings she had as she watched Mason with the children. He would make a good father, she thought. And a good husband, if he ever took a chance on love again.

"I'm going to marry you one day," the second little girl said, staring up at him now with large, sleepy blue eyes.

Mason smiled down at her. "Well, by the time you're old enough to get married, I'll be an old man."

She nodded. "Then I'll marry your child."

"I don't have any children."

She frowned, puckering her lower lip. "Why not?"

His expression contorted as he thought about his answer, no doubt wondering which answer would best cease the endless stream of questions that the girl was asking. "I'm not married. God wants people to get married first and then have children. That's His plan for us."

The little girl nodded, seemingly satisfied. Then she nuzzled her head into her chest. "God probably wants you to ask someone to marry you soon, then."

Mason looked up at Lexie, who pretended not to overhear. He wasn't smiling, she noticed as she flicked her gaze upward. Instead, he looked sad, she thought, as her heart tore just a little. She wondered if he was thinking about his late wife.

When the last child had gone, Clara found them in the hallway. She clasped her hands together joyfully. "Thank you two again. That was a huge help to me."

There was a sneaky twinkle in her eye, Lexie thought, smiling in return. If she didn't know better, she'd think Clara was hoping to create a spark between her and Mason. She peeked at him from the corner of her eye.

"Lunch?" Clara asked.

He shook his head, then leaned in and kissed the older woman's cheek. "Not today. I need to get to the fire station. They're shorthanded."

Clara's smile faded. Lexie felt the same way.

"Do you mind catching a ride back to the house with Clara and Rick?" he asked, glancing at her.

"No, of course not."

"Great." He headed out of the church, as if he couldn't wait to get out of there.

As if his life depended on it, Lexie thought. And for some reason, she knew it had nothing to do with his life or the fire, and everything to do with that little girl's comment in the nursery. The topic of marriage, as it related to him, seemed to have pressed on his nerves. His entire demeanor had changed.

Lexie stared after him, then turned as Clara reached for her hand.

"You can help me prepare lunch and we can start those cooking lessons we discussed the other day."

"I'd like that," Lexie said, forcing a smile. Her thoughts were still with the man she'd spent all morning with, and dinner last night, though.

Mason hopped in his truck and headed to the fire station, needing space and lots of it. He'd spent too much time with Lexie over the past few days and it was clouding his head. Chili, dinner, church. It was enough that he'd tossed and turned thinking about her last night, replaying every word of their conversation over dinner. Replaying her every smile and shy tilt of her chin.

Chief Rodriguez looked up as Mason came storming into the fire station. "What're you doing here? You're not on shift."

"I am now." The chief started to shake his head, but then a call came in over the radio. There was an accident on Highway 24. A woman was trapped inside a car with an infant in the back seat.

"Fine. Get suited up," the chief said, turning to Mason.

Adrenaline shot through his veins. These were his least favorite calls to go on. They hit too close to home. He'd been the one to arrive at Kristin's car accident first.

Memories came barreling into his mind as he climbed aboard the fire truck now. A second later, it shot forward out of the parking lot with its sirens warning oncoming traffic to stand back. The cars and trucks in front of them began to pull over along the side of the road, letting them pass. Hopefully the drivers inside were also lifting up a few prayers, Mason thought. Prayers were always appreciated.

On the day of Kristin's accident, Mason had arrived on the scene to find that she had a small cut on her forehead. She'd regained consciousness as he'd worked with several of the other men to help cut her out of her small sedan.

"Mason?" Her speech had been weak, confused, which was typical of a person who'd just been in a car accident. Kristin had never been in an accident before. She was in shock.

"You're fine. Just a little car accident," he'd told her, squeezing her hand softly. "I'll get you out and take you to the hospital."

An ambulance had already been waiting on the scene to do that. After a few minutes of work, her door had opened and he'd carefully moved her, calling on his fireman training, cautious just in case she had a neck injury. That had been his biggest concern at the time. They'd had an argument earlier that morning. It had momentarily occurred to him to apologize as he helped her to a stretcher. She'd been fading in and out of consciousness, though. He'd apologize later, after she'd been checked out by a doctor.

Mason had left the fire truck he'd driven in with another guy he worked with and climbed into the ambulance with his wife.

The driver of the other car had been rolled on a stretcher into a second ambulance. Mason remembered watching that poor guy, covered in blood, being carted away. He hadn't looked good. In Mason's profession, he saw a lot of things that weren't good. Too many things. But then there were times when he was able to help save a life. He wasn't disillusioned. He knew every life saved was only by God's grace. But Mason enjoyed being a part of that. It felt like his calling.

The fire truck stopped now and Mason got off, along with two other men. The car was smashed badly all around a woman in her mid-to-late twenties. She was crying hysterically, but her eyes were alert, unlike how Kristin's had been.

Mason glanced at the infant in the back car seat, too. The boy screamed and thrashed around, waving his little arms and kicking his legs. If the child was too seriously hurt, he wouldn't be doing that. "Let's get 'em out!" he called, acting quickly. He could already hear ambulances drawing near in the distance.

Ten minutes later, the woman was on a stretcher. Seeing her baby in one piece seemed to calm her considerably.

"Are you in any pain?" Mason asked.

"No." She shook her head.

"Try not to move," he reminded her. He watched as she was pushed into an ambulance and carried away. He'd check on her later, to make sure everything was fine.

Chief Rodriguez patted his back, and they both expelled a breath. "I don't know what brought you in today, but I'm grateful for your help, son."

Mason nodded. Lexie had been what had brought him in. He was getting too close to her, and today was just a reminder of why that was a bad idea for him. He'd had his chance at love, and it'd ended badly. He wasn't willing to go through that kind of pain again.

He returned to the station and worked for a few more hours and then headed to the Teen Center, hoping Lexie would be at the Carlyles' home. She usually only stopped by the center on weeknights.

"I heard you worked the accident today," Dave said, looking up as he walked into the Teen Center.

"Yeah."

"How'd it go?"

Mason plopped into a chair beside his friend. "I called and checked on the patient on the way here. She's fine. A couple of bruises, that's all."

Dave nodded. "Good." He stood up. "So what's bothering you?"

Mason shook his head. "Just tired."

"So go home," Dave said. "John and I are here tonight. We're going to play a board game or something with the kids and pop some corn."

Mason didn't budge.

"Oh. Wait. You're not going home because you're avoiding a certain houseguest that's starting to get under your skin."

Mason didn't argue. "You know as good as I do that I don't date."

"Maybe you should. It's been two years, buddy."

Mason's gaze sliced upward. "I know exactly how long it's been. And I'm not ready."

Dave held up his hands. "Okay. So I guess you'll be hiding out for the rest of the summer until she leaves town."

That sounded like a plan to Mason. The only problem was that Lexie was everywhere he turned. The Carlyles', the Teen Center, church. And now he'd gone and asked her to go on the camping trip with the kids. He'd practically begged her to chaperone, and she'd agreed. There was nowhere he could hide.

Chapter Nine

The health care clinic was packed for a Monday morning. Lexie took a breath as she looked out into the waiting room.

"What am I going to do when you leave at the end of the summer?" Dr. Marcus pondered. "The caseload has really picked up since we opened."

"I thought you were conducting interviews."

"Oh, I am. People don't exactly line up to work for peanuts, though. That's not why most people become doctors."

"It's rewarding work. Truly. I haven't felt this good in a long time," Lexie said.

"That can't be all due to helping here."

She grabbed a file and shrugged. "Clara's meals aren't hurting, either. She's even teaching me to cook."

Dr. Marcus grinned. "You could always stay. You'd beat out any applicant that applied for this job."

"Thanks for saying so," she said. But staying wasn't part of the plan. Grabbing a new folder, Lexie spotted Clara walking through the front door. "I'm pulling Clara Carlyle back now. She has an appointment."

Dr. Marcus looked up. "Everything okay?" he asked.

"Just an overdue checkup. I'll fill you in later."

"Good." He waved as Clara approached the front desk. "Great to see you, Clara."

Clara nodded. "It's awfully crowded in here today. Maybe I should come back at another time."

Lexie came around the counter and wrapped her arm around Clara's shoulders. "I knew you'd say that. Which is why I made you an appointment. You can come right on back."

"Oh. You already know me too well."

"Like family," Lexie said, thinking of what Mason had told her. She was beginning to think of Clara and Rick like family, too. She closed the door behind them, shutting them in the private room. "Any headaches today?"

"Not yet."

"Good. Let's see if your blood pressure has gone down since Saturday night." She placed a blood pressure cuff on Clara's upper arm and pressed the on button, waiting as it tightened. They sat quietly together as it inflated. Then Lexie frowned at the reading. "How long have you been having these headaches, Clara?" she asked, looking up.

"Oh, a few months."

Lexie shook her head. She'd heard the age-old complaint that men didn't like to go to the doctor, but she was shocked that a woman in her sixties didn't maintain her health. Especially since Clara took care of everyone else in her life.

"I'm concerned," Lexie said after several more assessments. "Really concerned." She sat on a swivel chair in front of Clara and narrowed her eyes. "How do you feel about medication?"

Clara's eyes widened. "I don't want to depend on a pill every day for the rest of my life."

"High blood pressure can be serious, though. You could have a number of consequences that are much worse than an occasional headache. High blood pressure can cause you to have a stroke, Clara."

Clara's eyes teared up. "Oh, dear."

Lexie reached for her hand. "Your blood pressure is only moderately high, but it's not something to ignore. Lots of people take medication to regulate their blood pressure."

Clara's chin quivered. "I'll pray about it."

Lexie nodded. "You definitely should, but I also really think we need to take medical action as soon as possible."

Clara shook her head, the wrinkles on her face multiplying as her look of disapproval grew. "Is there an alternative method for lowering my blood pressure? Other than taking medication?"

Lexie chewed her lower lip as she thought on her response. According to everything she'd learned in her training, Clara's blood pressure warranted medication. "Well, changes in your diet and exercise routine would help."

Clara smiled for the first time since walking into the examining room. "That sounds good to me. I'd rather start there."

It sounded good, but it was easier said than done, Lexie thought. Especially for someone who was set in their ways. "Okay. Well, I can help you with that." Lexie had been meaning to take time to start exercising anyway. It felt wrong to advise her patients to do something that she wasn't already doing herself. "We can meet up and go walking every afternoon."

"That would be nice, dear. Like a little visit for us girls."

Lexie grabbed her prescription pad and started writing. "Diet and exercise," she wrote. Ripping the paper off, she handed it to Clara. "We'll get started tonight."

It'd been a long day at the firehouse for Mason, and now here he was doing what some might call more work. He laid down the last box of equipment he'd unloaded from his truck and wiped at the perspiration on his forehead. The chili fund-raiser had been more profitable than he'd ever hoped for. They'd raised all the money needed to fund the trip. "All right, junior campers. What'll we need to do to get you guys ready for a weekend under the stars?"

Thirteen teenage faces stared back at him. As far as he knew, none of them had ever gone camping before. That was one of the points of making it happen this summer.

"We need to know how to pitch a tent," Max, a sixteen-year-old boy with a heart of platinum, offered up. Max lived with his father and took odd jobs around town to help pay the rent. Even though they were pressed for money at his home, he was always offering to do odd jobs for free when the opportunity arose. He was a good kid. Looking around, Mason thought that they were all great kids.

"If we want a shelter over our heads, that's something we need to learn," Mason agreed. He pulled up a metal fold-out chair and sat down.

"We should know how to collect sticks and make a fire," Andrew said.

Mason pointed at him. "Yes. We should make sure we bring our matches. And that we know about fire safety, too."

Dave started walking toward them from the office. He'd been on shift with Mason earlier today, and he looked just as happy to be here—home away from home. "We just got our forest fire under wraps, so let's go easy on making fires out in the woods, guys. It's summertime. We won't be cold."

"Well, how will we scare away the bears?" a teen named Megan asked.

Amber looked at her. "Bears?" she repeated, growing a shade whiter than her already pale skin.

Mason grinned. He was thrilled to see Amber here tonight. And despite himself, he was also thrilled to see the red-toned brunette keeping busy in the office, preparing a first aid kit for their camping trip. He knew that Lexie had put in as many hours at the health clinic today as he had at the fire department. Then she'd come straight here.

"Mr. Mason?" someone repeated.

Mason blinked and refocused his attention on Max. "Yeah? Sorry."

"I asked what we'll do for fun when we're camping."

Mason looked at Lexie again. He had fun every time she entered the room these days. He'd tried his best to keep his distance from her since church yesterday, but living on the same premises didn't make that easy. And Lexie was taking her role as camp chaperone seriously. She had no intention of just tagging along when they went camping. No, she was preparing things, and Mason had noticed that she'd checked out a stack of books on wilderness survival. The woods of Carolina Shores weren't exactly the wilderness, but he admired Lexie's enthusiasm. "Fun is a frame of mind. You can have fun doing anything," he told the kids.

The teens weren't impressed by his answer. They blinked, stone-faced, back at him.

"We were able to purchase some fishing poles with the money we raised at the chili fund-raiser," he added. "We also got some Frisbees and footballs to toss around."

The kids cheered now.

"Ms. Kristin would've liked this," Luke, one of the older kids in the group, said. He'd been the one to take Kristin's death the hardest. He'd stopped coming to the Teen Center for a while, until Mason and Dave had gone to visit him at his home. He'd never lost anyone in his life. He'd felt betrayed by Kristin, and by God. For a long time, he'd been confused. Now, he did what he could to keep Kristin's memory alive. He'd been the one to suggest putting Kristin's picture up in the back of the building, so that everyone could see who had started this place.

"Yes, she would've loved this idea." Mason's heart ached for a moment. He glanced down to the floor to check his emotions, then returned his gaze to Luke. "She was scared of snakes, though. Terrified of them, actually, so she would've been hesitant to come along with us."

"Snakes?" Amber asked. Apparently his little homeless teen didn't like critters of the wild, either. He guessed that meant she wasn't staying in the woods at the moment. Her story was still that she lived with her uncle outside of town, even though she'd taken a shower here this afternoon and she'd accepted a new outfit from the donations pile.

"It's very unlikely that one will get in with you in your sleeping bag," Dave teased the group.

Mason gave him a hard stare. He needed this girl to not back out of camping with them. The more time he spent with her, the more he hoped she'd trust him. A teen belonged with a family, blood-related or not. She didn't need to be on her own and fending for herself in the wild.

"Snakes are more scared of you than you are of them," Dave added, in an effort to ease the discomfort.

"We got each of you a sleeping bag, too," Mason said, gesturing at the pile of equipment on the floor. "Next weekend is going to be a great trip."

"What about the forest fire?" Megan asked.

"It's all but out. And we'll be miles away from where it was," Dave answered. "No worries about that. Plus—" he grinned "—you'll be with Carolina Shores's top-notch firemen. No worries there."

As Dave continued talking to the teens, Mason glanced toward the office where Lexie was again. She looked up and met his gaze, catching him watching her this time. "I'll be right back, guys," Mason said, his legs moving before his brain had approved his actions. Next thing he knew he was leaning against the door frame to the office, face-to-face with Lexie. "Hi."

Her cheeks blushed a little, which he found curious. "You haven't changed your mind about helping us with the camping trip next weekend, have you?" he asked, knowing that she hadn't.

"I'm a woman of my word." She smiled. "And I'm actually looking forward to it."

"Good." He nodded. And despite himself, he was looking forward to the trip, too. Partly because he'd be spending more time with her, which was insane. He wasn't interested in dating or relationships. His plate was full with other obligations and commitments. Obligations and commitments that wouldn't be disappearing at the end of the summer. Lexie would be disappearing, though. "I need to make sure you know exactly what you're agreeing to. There's no air-conditioning. No bathrooms." He cocked an eyebrow.

Lexie grimaced. "Sounds brutal," she said, teasingly. "I can handle that, though. There is one deal-breaker for me going on this trip."

"Oh, yeah? What's that?" Worry niggled in his chest. He really wanted her to go on this camping trip with the group. He hadn't looked forward to something like this in a very long time, and that was, in part, thanks to her.

"Coffee. Will we be able to make coffee?" she asked, with all the seriousness of a house fire.

"I'll make sure of it."

Her shoulders relaxed. "Phew. I like to think of myself as a simple girl, but I don't get far in the mornings without my first cup of caffeine."

Mason laughed, tossing a glance over his shoulder. "Looks like Amber is making herself at home here."

Lexie followed his gaze. "She's such a sweet girl. I can't imagine why she ran away from home."

"Me, neither." Mason watched the sullen-faced teen's expression light up as Dave heaved a sleeping bag in her direction. "I'm praying God will lower her guard between now and next weekend, though, so we can find out."

Lexie nodded. "Me, too. Speaking of which, we're going to be missing church while we're on the trip. Any plans for that?"

Mason folded his arms. "I thought I'd bring a Bible and maybe do a little reading from it. Why? Do you have something else in mind?" He liked the way her eyes sparkled when she got excited.

Lexie lifted a shoulder. "I thought it might be fun to pick a reading that related to what we'll be doing out there. Jesus did a lot of fishing like we'll be doing. Or it might be fun to read about David and Goliath and have the kids make sling shots. Not to kill anything, of course, but…"

Mason grinned. "I love that idea. I'm glad you agreed to come along with us." His voice dropped as he spoke to her and the room seemed to grow smaller. "I don't really think we could do this without you."

Her gaze lifted and met his, holding him hostage.

There was something between him and Lexie. He'd tried to ignore it, fight it, but now maybe he was interested in exploring it further.

"Hey, Mason. A little assistance with the tents over here!" Dave called at him from behind.

Lexie looked away. "You're needed." She laughed.

"Right. I'll, uh, see you back at Clara and Rick's later?" he asked hopefully.

She nodded. "Yes. My home away from home, away from home." A small laugh escaped her lips.

"Good," he said, forcing his feet to move away from Lexie. Because his heart was telling him to draw closer.

Lexie sat up and glanced at her watch. She was meeting Clara in five minutes to go on their new evening routine of walking to lower Clara's blood pressure. After bending to tighten the bow on her sneakers, she headed down the hall where Clara was waiting for her.

"I'm ready!" Clara called, dressed in an oversize T-shirt and a pair of sweatpants.

Lexie nodded. "Me, too."

"Now, I'm a little tired today, so bear with me, dear."

"Don't worry about that. I'll match your pace. We're in no hurry," Lexie said.

As they walked, Clara did most of the talking. She was interested in pointing out different houses and mentioning who lived in them this evening, which Lexie found curious.

"Other than the hospital staff," Clara said, "Dr. Marcus is the only doctor in Carolina Shores, you know. We don't have any private doctors' offices."

Lexie nodded. "Dr. Marcus is planning to hire someone else for the clinic. He'll be doing interviews soon. I think he already has several scheduled."

Clara watched her as they walked, their steps in sync with one another. "And will you be interviewing with him?" she asked.

Clara was anything but subtle.

"I have interviews lined up in Raleigh at the end of the summer." One of which was all but a sure hire for her. Her parents knew the physician. It was a prestigious position where she'd learn a lot and set herself up to be one of the leading general medicine practitioners one day.

"Doesn't hurt to keep your options open," Clara chimed, walking with a little pep in her step suddenly. "I hear you're going with Mason on that camping trip next weekend," Clara said then.

"With Mason and all the teens at the Teen Center," Lexie added. "They do several trips a year," Lexie reminded her, as if Clara didn't already know. "Mason thinks it'd be more comfortable for some of the girls if there was a female chaperone along with them, in addition to the guys from the fire department."

"And I'm sure he wants you to come along for reasons other than chaperoning. He seems to enjoy your presence during dinners at night. And you two handled the nursery like a couple of pros last week."

"We're just friends, Clara," Lexie said, seeing exactly where her bighearted, matchmaker hostess was going with the conversation.

"Uh-huh."

"Really. Mason needs a girlfriend about as badly as I need a new fiancé."

"That's exactly what I was thinking." Clara winked and then came to an abrupt stop at a ranch-style brick home near the end of the street.

"What are we doing? Are you all right?" Lexie asked, growing concerned as she inspected Clara outwardly.

Her breathing seemed fine. They'd only walked half a mile so far, and Clara was showing no signs of physical distress. "Do you need to take a rest break?"

Clara started walking down the driveway toward the house's front door. "I think a rest break would be lovely, dear."

"Clara?"

As they got closer, Clara's shoulders slumped. She glanced over at Lexie, who had closed the distance between them. "I told Elaine Dunklemeyer from church that you were helping me with my headaches. Turns out Elaine's been having some ailments of her own. I thought you might take a look-see at her while we're down this way." Clara didn't wait for Lexie to respond before continuing down the driveway and pressing the doorbell.

Lexie glanced at her attire. She was a doctor. She didn't treat people wearing sweat shorts and sneakers.

A second later, the door opened and a small woman with silver hair smiled back at them. She motioned for them to come in, despite Lexie's unprofessional dress.

Elaine led them inside the house and motioned at some cookies on the coffee table. "They're homemade. Just for you."

"You knew we were coming?" Lexie asked, glancing at Clara again. She'd have to have a talk with Clara about this later.

"Of course, dear. I've been waiting anxiously for your visit all day. I'm so glad there's another doctor in the area."

"You can come see Dr. Marcus and me at the new health care clinic anytime," Lexie said.

"Oh, the thought of going into some cold clinic where no one knows me and waiting for hours just gives me the creeps."

Lexie couldn't help but laugh. "The creeps?"

"Well, yes. Everyone's so rushed and no one really cares about you. You're just a number there."

"Well, you haven't been to our clinic yet, Mrs. Dunklemeyer," Lexie responded, surprising herself by using the word *our*. That's how she'd begun to feel about the clinic in the short time she'd been there, though. It might be harder than she thought to walk away at the end of the summer. "So what seems to be the problem?" she asked, shaking those thoughts away. Staying in Carolina Shores wasn't an option. Like Clara had said, there was only the hospital and the health care clinic. Not much opportunity. And she couldn't stay at the Carlyles' indefinitely. This wasn't her home.

Even if it was starting to feel that way.

Lexie scanned her eyes over Elaine's body. Outwardly, the older woman seemed perfectly healthy, with the exception of being a tad overweight.

Elaine raised her sleeve, revealing a small rash.

Lexie leaned forward to inspect it. "Does it itch?" she asked.

"A little."

Lexie nodded. The rash was pink, not red. They were small bumps, barely raised. "How long have you had it?"

"About a week."

"Do you have it anywhere else on your body?" Lexie asked.

Elaine proceeded to point out other areas.

"Have you changed your laundry detergent lately? Changed soaps?"

Elaine shook her head slowly, still thinking about her answer. "Well…" She chewed her bottom lip. "Would that cause this rash?"

Lexie smiled. "What did you change?"

"My husband, Bob, got me a new bubble bath last week. It smells so good and it was such a thoughtful gift. Smells like my mother's kitchen growing up. Vanilla."

"I see. Why don't you put the bubble bath away for about a week? See if the rash doesn't resolve itself. If it doesn't, you come see me at the health care clinic and I'll take another look. I promise you you'll be more than a number there."

Elaine nodded quickly. "Thank you so much. Really." She lowered her sleeve. "That rash has been worrying me all week. To think it could be from something as simple as my bubble bath." She looked at Clara. "Who'd have guessed?"

Clara shrugged. "It's good to have a doctor around, isn't it?"

"It sure is," Elaine agreed. Then she collected a piece of Tupperware and began to load the cookies on the coffee table into it. "You're taking these home with you. As a thank-you gift. And if there's anything I can do, just let me know. I've got a green thumb. I can help in your garden."

Lexie bit into one of the cookies, catching the crumbs as they fell with her free hand. "I don't have a garden, but thank you. Just come see me at the clinic if the rash doesn't go away." She stood.

"Oh, I will. Thank you," Elaine said again, walking them to the door. "Take good care of our doctor friend, Clara. See if you can make her stick around," she whispered loud enough for Lexie to hear.

"I'm working on it," Clara whispered back.

"Sorry, dear," Clara said as they walked back home in the fading daylight. "You've just helped me so much. When Elaine told me about her ailment, I thought you wouldn't mind doing a quick check."

"I don't. But next time refer people to the clinic. Dr. Marcus is there to help me if I need it."

"Right. I'll do that." Clara fanned her face as they walked.

"Are you too hot?" Lexie asked.

"No. Exercise is good. I should've been doing this all along." She glanced over. "It won't be nearly as fun after you go home, though. I'll have to get a new walking partner."

"A partner helps keep up the motivation," Lexie agreed.

Clara nodded. "I think this diet and exercise prescription will work well for me."

"Good. Why don't you come back to the clinic next week so we can check your vitals again, though? I want to keep an eye on you."

Clara tsked. "Here I thought I was helping you this summer."

"You are. I can never repay your kindness," Lexie said.

"That's the thing about kindness, dear. It's not meant to be paid back. Just paid forward."

Lexie smiled. Clara reminded her so much of her grandma Jean. Lexie may have been good at doling out medical advice, but Clara and her grandmother's advice soothed the spirit. "I can do that," she said.

Chapter Ten

The next afternoon Mason set the receiver down at the fire station and frowned.

"What's wrong?" Dave asked, walking in and looking at him.

"Nothing," Mason said. "The air quality is good over at Chesterfield Estates and the neighboring areas. We can let all of the residents move back in. No danger." Some of the residents had already moved back, but many of the people in Chesterfield were elderly and had health conditions that made them more susceptible to environmental pollution. It wasn't recommended for them to return home. And Lexie had been discouraged from going home because of her asthma.

"And this is bad because…?" Dave grinned.

"What are you talking about? It's great news." Mason couldn't make his voice fake the enthusiasm, though.

"Lexie will be thrilled to move out of the Carlyles' place, I'm sure."

Mason nodded. "Yeah. I thought I'd run over there and tell her myself."

Dave shrugged. "It's slow around here. You should. Try to smile when you break the news to her, though.

Make it seem like you're not depressed about the fact that she won't be a couple yards from you every day anymore."

Mason shot him a look. "It's not like that, and you know it."

Dave held up his hands. "I don't know anything. And would it be so bad if it *were* like that?"

Mason refused to answer that question because the truth was he liked Lexie. More and more every day. "She's only here for the summer."

"Plans change. You and I both know it." Dave's gaze softened and Mason immediately knew what he was thinking. Things didn't always work out like we wanted them to.

"Yeah." Mason headed toward the door. "I'll see you later tonight."

Mason climbed into his truck and headed toward Clara and Rick's house. Lexie's rental home being available to live in again was good news, he reminded himself. She'd be happy. And they'd still see each other at church and the Teen Center. She was going camping with them this weekend.

He swallowed. Dave was right. His feelings for Lexie had gotten a little deeper than he'd expected. It was only natural. He was a single man and Lexie was as smart as she was pretty, and as nice as she was giving. It didn't mean that things between them were lasting. She was here for a few more weeks, and that was all. Then life as it'd been before Lexie came to town would return to normal.

"Mason," Lexie said, standing beside Clara as he pulled in. They were dressed in T-shirts and sweat shorts, with a thin layer of sweat making their faces glow.

"I thought you had to work tonight," Clara said, pulling a towel to her cheek.

"I do. I am. Are you two exercising?" he asked.

"Walking buddies," Clara confirmed. "This is day two of Lexie here whipping me into shape." She laughed jollily.

"Oh, good. Means you'll still be coming around," he said, connecting eyes with Lexie. Sweat didn't detract from her appeal. The guy who'd walked out on marrying her must've been blind.

"Still come around after what?" She folded her arms around her. Since he'd met her, he'd never known her to do anything for herself. She volunteered all her time. He suspected that's what she was doing with Clara by exercising with her. Lexie was already in good shape.

"After you move back into your rental home. The air quality is normal. There's no more risk to residents."

"Oh." Lexie nodded her head, her gaze falling to her athletic shoes.

He waited for her to smile. Waited for her to jump up and down.

"Something wrong?" he asked, hoping despite himself that she was as disappointed as he was.

She shook her head. "I guess I've probably overstayed my welcome here anyway. This is good news."

"No, this is terrible news," Clara said, holding a hand to her cheek. "I like Lexie living here."

"Aww. That's sweet of you, and I've really enjoyed being here, as well. But I guess I should probably go back. I already paid rent for the summer. I'm obligated and there's no reason to waste a perfectly good house. Someone else might need your guest room."

Clara's eyebrows dipped with worry. "Will you still be my walking buddy?"

"Of course I will." Lexie wrapped her arms around Clara's shoulders. "But no more house calls like last night, okay?" She narrowed her eyes and Clara laughed ruefully.

"Deal." Clara beamed at her.

Lexie turned to look at Mason. "Thanks for letting me know."

"No problem. The fire station is slow right now if you want me to help you bring your stuff over to your rental."

"Right now?" she asked, her mouth falling open.

"So soon?" Clara fretted.

"Or I can help you another day this week if you'd rather," he offered.

"It's just a few bags. And now is as good a time as any, I guess." Lexie sighed and forced a smile, but it didn't reach her pretty green eyes. "I can get it myself."

"I'll go just in case," he said. "Sometimes evacuated neighborhoods are victims of looters. I'd feel better about it if I went and checked things out for you."

Lexie nodded. "Okay. I'll be quick. Thank you." She started toward the Carlyles' house.

Mason watched her go.

"I don't want her to leave, either," Clara commented. She laid a hand on his shoulder. "At least she's staying in Carolina Shores a little longer, though, right? I'll dislike it more when she goes back home. To her real home." Clara seemed to consider that thought for a long moment. "You never know, though."

"Plans change," he said, remembering his conversation with Dave back at the fire department.

"That's right. God's plans for us are better than anything we could ever envision for ourselves."

Despite his past, Mason knew that was true. God's plans were better than his own. Mason wondered what

God's plans were for Lexie. He wanted her to be happy, whether she was here or in Raleigh.

Lexie grabbed the last thing in the guest room closet—her grandmother's wedding dress. She folded the dress, covered by a clean upside-down black trash bag, and placed it inside her suitcase. This dress was what brought her here in the first place. If she'd never gone back for it, she wouldn't have met Mason or the Carlyles. Things had worked out just the way they were supposed to. Looking around to make sure she had everything, she walked out and back toward her car.

"I'll follow you over," Mason said when she exited through the screen door.

"Thank you, Mason. For everything. I don't think I ever really thanked you for rescuing me when I broke through the evacuation barriers. And for not having me arrested."

Mason stepped closer. "I'm just glad God put me in the right place at the right time. I don't want to think about what would've happened if no one had come along."

She swallowed the thick knot in her throat. "You also told Clara and Rick about me. I wouldn't have had a place to stay if not for you."

"I didn't know Clara would offer you a place to stay, though. I don't get credit for that." He shook his head.

"Anyway, my summer would've gone up in flames if not for you." She stepped closer, went up on her tiptoes and, without thinking, kissed his cheek. It was an innocent gesture, one she would've done to anyone who'd saved her life and her summer mentorship. Mason wasn't just anyone, though. As she returned to flat feet, her cheeks burned. She had feelings for this man that seemed to grow every time she was with him. "So I guess we better get going so you can get back to work."

"Right." There was an unmistakable look on Mason's face. He'd been affected by the kiss just now, as well. "I'll, uh, see you there."

A few minutes later, she pulled into the driveway of her rental home and saw Mason pull up behind her in the rearview mirror.

"The scene of the crime," Mason joked as he stepped toward her.

She breathed a sigh of relief that things weren't weird between them. Good. She just needed to never kiss Mason again. They were only friends and that's how it had to stay.

"I'll go in first and check things out," he said.

Lexie nodded. "Do you have a weapon? In case someone has broken in?"

"Don't need one. Usually looters take what they want and disappear. And it's doubtful anyone's been here. I just wanted to make sure for your safety."

Lexie watched Mason unlock her front door and disappear inside. She hugged her arms around her body, suddenly nervous. She was glad Mason had come here with her. He was a lifesaver in more ways than one. And a really good friend that she didn't want to lose.

Her breath caught when she saw movement out of the corner of her eye. A girl slipped out the back door, leaving it open. She had long, ash-blond hair.

"Amber?" Lexie's legs started running before her mind had processed the situation. Amber had been inside the house when Mason entered. She was sneaking out the back now and attempting to disappear before he caught her staying there. "Amber?" Lexie called, running after her. "Amber, wait!"

Amber had a duffel bag on her shoulder. She didn't turn back, but disappeared through the woods instead.

Lexie started to chase after her, but stopped when Mason called her name.

"What's wrong? I heard you yelling. What happened?" he asked, coming down the porch steps.

Lexie turned, holding a hand to her chest. "You didn't see her?"

"See who?" he asked, hurrying toward her.

"Amber was inside. She's been living here."

Mason's gaze narrowed and then he took off running toward the woods. "Stay put. I'll see if I can catch her," he called behind him.

Lexie waited a moment and then went inside the house. The rental home had telltale signs of life. There was a half-eaten sandwich on the kitchen table. Most of the food she'd loaded the refrigerator with on her first night here was gone. She didn't mind. She was glad that Amber had food to eat. The fact that she was staying here, though, meant that Amber had lied. She wasn't living with family. It also meant she'd been breaking the law by breaking and entering. And stealing.

Sadness pierced Lexie's heart. She turned toward a sound behind her and met Mason's worried stare.

"You couldn't find her?" she asked.

"She's good at disappearing." He looked around the room, then ran his hands through his hair in frustration. "This probably means she won't be coming back to the Teen Center. Her jig is up."

Lexie walked to him and put her hand on his shoulder. "You're worried about her. I am, too. What can we do?"

The muscle of Mason's jaw pulsed. "I can call the local police to keep a lookout for her. I don't want them to arrest her, though. That won't help anything." He shook his head. "All we can do is pray that she turns up."

Two nights later, Mason was at the Teen Center, on high alert every time the door opened. Amber hadn't shown up since they'd discovered her at Lexie's rental home.

The door opened again. Mason leaned forward, hoping it was Amber. He wasn't disappointed when the person walking in turned out to be Lexie, though. She was becoming more and more of a regular at the center; she showed a couple nights a week after her evening walks with Clara. She was still wearing her tennis shoes and her hair pulled back in a loose ponytail tonight.

"How's it feel to be in your own place?" he asked as she came and sat beside him.

She shrugged. "Lonely. I've realized that I like the noise of other people close by."

He nodded. "I know what you mean. You'll still see a lot of Clara and Rick, though. With your walks and dinner. And church."

"I had dinner with them tonight before heading over. And—" Lexie shook her head "—Clara handed me a schedule for keeping nursery over the next few weeks. Turns out that the children have requested for us to come back."

"Us?" Mason drew back.

Lexie laughed, holding up her hands. "Don't worry. Clara knows better than to put you on the official schedule. Plus, she has no idea when you're on call at the fire station. It's just me." She cocked a brow. "But you can feel free to help out anytime, scheduled or not. I'd rather have backup when caring for a handful of active toddlers."

Mason shrugged. "Maybe I will. It wasn't so bad."

Even though one of the little girl's comments about getting married had completely thrown him. He'd heard that kids said the oddest things, but his heart had taken a hit with that one. He'd been married once and he didn't intend to go down that road again.

Lexie locked a loose strand of her hair behind her ear and pressed her lips together as if she was holding in what she wanted to say.

"What?" he asked. "You're trying to figure out how to ask me something." He grinned. "I'm not only an expert firefighter, I'm good at reading people's body language, too. What is it?"

Her shoulders slumped. "Dinner. As you know, Clara and I haven't just been walking together. We've been cooking together, too, sometimes. Healthy cooking."

He nodded. "I've noticed her meals have been a little different lately. They're good. Healthy eating is good, right?"

Lexie rolled her lips again. "So, I've been wanting to find a way to thank you for all that you've done for me this summer."

He put down the events calendar he'd been looking at for the center and gave her his full attention. "You know you don't have to thank me. Helping people is my job."

She held up a hand. "You've gone above and beyond the duties of your job. I already spoke to Dave and he said you weren't going to be here or at the fire station tomorrow night."

Mason nodded. He usually took one or two nights off a week to clear his head.

"I'd like you to consider coming to dinner at my place. I want to cook for you," she said quickly. Then she sucked in a breath. "I want to cook you a thank-you meal."

His heart lit up at the thought of having Lexie cook for

him. She wasn't asking him on a date. It was a thank-you meal. "I thought you said you couldn't cook," he said.

"I'm learning. So—"

He nodded. "I'll be there. Sounds good."

"Okay. Great." Standing, she started to go back out to the community area where several of the kids were. "Then it's a date. Not a date," she corrected, turning back. "A plan. It's a plan."

Mason contained a smile. "I can't wait," he said, meaning it. In fact, he hadn't meant anything so much in a very long time. "Can I bring something?" he asked. "A beverage? Dessert?"

"Just bring yourself," she said. "I'll handle everything else."

"I can do that." He watched her leave to go hang out with the kids, who seemed as happy in her presence as he was. She was a ray of sunshine wherever she went. Lexie never complained and she always worked hard at whatever she did. There were so many qualities to admire about the woman, which was exactly what he was doing: admiring her, nothing else. The little girl at the nursery was wrong. Marriage wasn't in his future. Neither was dating. The only thing in his immediate future was a thank-you dinner at Lexie's house. And he couldn't wait to attend.

Chapter Eleven

Lexie cooked with her cell phone on speaker. "The air in my neighborhood is fine, Mom," she said for the tenth time on this call. "But I have an inhaler in case I have an attack. I am a doctor after all."

"But I'm your mother."

Lexie poked at the still-frozen chicken thawing in her sink. It'd been sitting there for over an hour and still seemed like one big block of pink ice. She opened the microwave door and plopped the chicken breast inside, trying to remember how Clara thawed her meats.

"If the air quality starts to get bad again, I can always return to the Carlyles' house."

"Or you could come home. We miss you. Your grandmother misses you, too."

Lexie smiled, watching the microwave timer count down in neon green numbers. She glanced at her clock. Mason would be here soon and she hadn't even started cooking yet. "I miss you guys, too." Emotion hit her all of a sudden. At home she visited her grandma Jean several times a week. They shared tea and Lexie listened to her stories, even if she'd heard them a thousand times already.

"I'll call Grandma tomorrow. Tell her I love her. I love you and Dad, too, Mom."

They chatted for a few more minutes, then Lexie hung up and pulled the chicken out of the microwave. It had thawed on the gristly edges, but it was still hard. She took a deep breath and dialed Clara's number. No answer. She was probably out on her daily walk, which Lexie had opted out of today in order to make sure this thank-you dinner for Mason was a success.

It definitely wasn't turning out to be a success.

"Think, Lexie, think." She'd survived medical school. How hard could it be to cook one little chicken breast?

The doorbell rang and Lexie jumped, trying not to panic.

She sucked in a shaky breath and glanced back at the stove before heading down the hall to the front door. Mason was going to think she was incompetent. No man wanted to be involved with a woman who couldn't cook. Not that she wanted Mason as anything more than a friend.

She opened the door and forced a shaky smile.

"What's the matter?" he asked, stepping inside.

Her smile wilted. He wasn't kidding when he said he read people's body language well. "What do you mean?" Her words squeaked out on raw nerves. Then tears began to collect in her eyes.

Mason shut the door behind him, turning to study her again. "Your face is all flush and your eyes are glassy. Are you upset about something?" he asked.

"I… I've just been standing over a hot stove." Which was the truth, but it wasn't the main reason she was suddenly a mess.

"Oh." His eyes brightened and he rubbed his hands

together. "So what's for dinner? I've been looking forward to this thank-you meal all day."

One tear slipped down her cheek, and then another. Then her head fell to her chest in breathless sobs. She tried to answer his question. Tried to spit out any words that might convince him that she was fine, but all she could do was cry.

She wasn't fine. She pulled her hands over her face, wishing that she could disappear under her bedroom covers. She was a frustrated, incapable, homesick mess all of a sudden.

Mason led her to the couch and waited. He patted her back and whispered some comforting words she couldn't hear through her tears. Then, when the stove began to beep, he followed the sound to the kitchen. Lexie heard him opening cabinets and rummaging for where she kept her pots and pans. She heard his soft whistle as he worked. He was cooking their dinner, she realized.

She pressed her forehead deeper into her trembling hands. She'd ruined dinner, and more disappointing than that, Mason was going to think she was a crazy person. What was wrong with her?

She went to the bathroom in the hallway and looked at herself in the mirror. After taking a few calming breaths, the ruddiness of her skin began to return to normal. She fanned the air in front of her eyes to dry her tears, then said a silent prayer. She usually tried to stay calm in the presence of others. Even after Todd had told her he didn't want to get married anymore, she'd waited to dissolve into a puddle of tears until he'd left. She'd waited until she informed her family that the wedding was off, until she was in her Raleigh apartment and certain that no one would be interrupting her. Then she'd cried. Tonight she'd been unable to help herself, even though she'd known Mason would be arriving any minute. This wasn't like her at all.

Get it together, Lexie, she told herself. She liked Mason. She didn't want to scare him off. After a few more minutes, she left the bathroom and quietly tiptoed down the hall, pausing as Mason turned to look at her.

"It's nearly done." He offered a small smile, scanning his gaze over her as if to make sure she was okay. Then he turned back to the stove.

She sat at the kitchen table and took another slow, steadying breath to calm her racing thoughts. "I'm sorry," she finally said. "I wanted to cook you dinner. Not vice versa."

He lifted two plates off the counter and laid them down on the table.

"Spaghetti?"

"The chicken wasn't thawed. And I'm good at spaghetti, so…is this all right?" he asked. "If not I can try my hand at something else. Or I can run out and grab some fast food and bring it back."

"No. This is perfect." She submitted to a small chuckle.

"Glad to see you're feeling better."

She nodded. "Temporary insanity."

"You didn't look insane to me." His blue eyes were warm as he met her gaze. "You looked like someone who's been through a lot over the last couple months."

Her eyes burned, threatening to yield more tears. "Yeah. This summer has been quite an adventure." She gestured to the food. "We should eat while it's still hot. Do you mind saying the prayer?" she asked. Because the more she spoke, the more likely she was to start crying again. Her emotions were on high alert right now.

"Sure." Mason bowed his head and prayed, thanking God for the day, the food and the good company. "Amen."

The first few minutes were filled with forks tapping the plate as they swirled their noodles.

"Thanks again for coming. I'm sorry about…earlier." Her cheeks burned as she reminded him of her sobbing episode.

He shrugged. "No need to apologize. I'm sure I'll cry, too, when I leave the Carlyles' home."

Her brow furrowed. "That's not why I was crying."

"No? Don't tell me it's just about dinner? Because you could have served up charcoal and I'd have been happy."

She hesitated. "No." Her fork tapped the plate as she swirled her spaghetti and let it dangle in front of her. "I'm a little homesick, I guess." She felt him watching her. "I left Raleigh because I needed space. Then I spoke to my mother on the phone and…" She shook her head.

"And the space suddenly felt like one big crater?" he asked.

She smiled. "A little. More so now that I'm no longer in Clara and Rick's guest room." She waved a hand. "It's fine. I'm fine. Just being silly." She sniffled.

"It's not so silly, if you ask me."

"I actually feel a little guilty. I like my life here, as much or more than I do the life I led back home."

He nodded. "This town sure needs you while we have you. We'll miss you when you go back."

He didn't exactly say *he'd* miss her, but the look in his eyes implied it. She'd miss him, too. He was one of her favorite people in Carolina Shores.

"I didn't expect to fall in love with this place. I'm going to miss it here," she said softly. She'd fallen in love with everything about this town, including its people.

"It's only a two-hour drive. Clara will insist you come visit from time to time. And the kids at the Teen Center would like that, too."

Lexie wondered if Mason would want her to visit him. "Maybe Clara will let me stay in her guest room for old time's sake." She looked at their finished plates. "I do have dessert to offer you."

"Did you make it?" he asked.

She shook her head. "No. You're safe." With a laugh she rose from the table and retrieved an apple pie from the refrigerator. Cutting two slices and depositing them on two small dishes, she hooked her head. "Let's go sit on the back porch," she said. Fresh air always made her feel better. So did pie.

She led Mason to the screened porch off the back of the house, where a chorus of crickets serenaded them as they conversed. About their childhoods, about life, and loss.

"As much as I'd like to, I can't stay forever." Mason smiled as he gazed on her.

The dimly lit night made sharing a glance with him feel more intimate somehow. Lexie shivered.

"We have a camping trip tomorrow, bright and early. We both probably need to get some shut-eye. But thank you for dinner, Lexie."

"I should be thanking you." She shook her head. "I'll cook next time."

He stood and she followed him to the front door. "How about next time I just take you out to dinner?" He turned to look at her with his hand on the doorknob.

Her heart nearly knocked her down with its leap. He hadn't meant on a date. Of course he hadn't. Every meal they'd ever shared together had been for some other reason. She steadied her thoughts. "Sounds nice."

He tipped his head and started to walk down the driveway toward his truck. "See you tomorrow at sunrise."

"Looking forward to it," she said. Then she watched him get inside his truck and disappear into the night.

The next morning, Mason climbed behind the wheel and headed to Chesterfield Estates. He couldn't remember the last time he'd had an entire weekend off from the fire department. He and three of the firemen he worked with, who also volunteered at the Teen Center, packed up their respective trucks with equipment and all the food that fourteen hungry teens could possibly eat in two days. Dave was in charge of driving the bus that the church had loaned them for the occasion. Mason didn't envy him for having that job, chauffeuring around rowdy teens.

Instead, Mason was chauffeuring Lexie, which felt equally dangerous for very different reasons.

He honked the horn just outside her house, then stepped out to help her with her bags as she lugged them down the porch.

"I'm impressed," he said. "I half expected you to pack everything you own for the trip. I'm sure that's what the girls are doing."

His smile flattened as he mentioned the teen girls. Lexie's did, too. There were three girls going on the trip, but there should've been four. No one had seen or heard from Amber since Lexie had moved back into her rental home, though. Amber was gone.

He loaded Lexie's bag into the back of the truck and opened the passenger-side door for her. His mother had taught him to do that for all women, not just the ones he liked—the ones he liked more each time he saw them. "We'll go wait at the Teen Center parking lot for everyone to arrive," he said, pulling back out of her driveway. "Then we'll ride together as a group."

"Sounds good." Lexie was quiet for a long moment.

"About last night," she finally said. "I'm sorry for breaking down on you like that."

"I'm not. I was beginning to think that nothing got to you. It's okay to show your vulnerabilities. I was happy to be there for you."

"Thanks." She fidgeted with her hands in her lap. "I really wish Amber hadn't disappeared on us. Someone should be there for her."

Mason slowed down at the Teen Center parking lot, where several other cars were already gathered. "Have you been praying about it?" he asked.

Lexie nodded. "Of course."

He pointed to a girl standing off to the side. No one seemed to have noticed her yet. "Looks like your prayers were answered."

Lexie gasped, then grabbed the door handle and started hurrying toward Amber. He watched her pull the girl into a tight hug, which was exactly what Kristin would've done.

"I hope this means you'll be joining us on the trip," he said, approaching the two a moment later.

"If it's still okay," Amber said, not quite meeting his gaze.

"Of course it is," Lexie said. "Right, Mason?"

Amber twisted her mouth to one side as she looked up. "Did you call the cops on me?" the girl asked.

Lexie folded her arms at her chest. "No need. You are a friend of mine, and you can stay in my home anytime you need. I mean that."

Amber's guard softened. "Thanks." She looked at Mason. "I guess I'll go camping with you guys, then. I'm pretty good at pitching tents and stuff now. I can show the others a few things about outdoor survival, too, as long as there are no snakes and bears."

He wanted to ask how she knew about outdoor survival, where she'd been staying since she left Lexie's and why she couldn't go home. Those were all questions he hoped to have answers to by the end of the weekend. The last thing he wanted to do right now was frighten her off again. "Sounds great. So let's get this show on the road," he said instead.

Ten minutes later, with all the kids in the bus and the equipment loaded in the trucks, they took to the roads, heading to the camp site.

"I am so excited," Lexie said, seated beside him for the trip. "This is going to be the best trip ever."

Her enthusiasm was contagious. "It already is. Amber showed up, and you're here, too."

"Do you think we'll get through to her this weekend?"

"Only if she wants us to. Maybe she's feeling a little homesick, too." He glanced over at Lexie, remembering last night when she had been inconsolable for a few minutes. There was no way she wasn't going back to Raleigh in a few weeks, not when she missed her hometown that much. That meant these feelings that had started to spring up inside him needed to be squelched, like little fires that threatened to turn into an uncontrolled blaze.

Losing someone was hard; he knew that firsthand. His heart couldn't take another hit like that.

An hour later, he parked and looked over at a sleeping Lexie. The coffee he'd bought her on the way hadn't worked to keep her awake. Which was fine by him. He'd taken the time to clear his head and put his thoughts about his passenger in perspective. At least he'd tried to do that.

"Lexie?" He tapped her shoulder gently. "We're here. Lex?" He watched her stir, her eyelids slowly fluttering open.

With a yawn and stretch, she sat up and looked out

the window. Then she turned to him. "Into the wild," she said, opening her door and getting out.

He waited a second to extinguish those pesky sparks lighting up his heart again. They were deep in the woods now, and he'd already put out one forest fire this summer.

She tapped on the driver's-side window. "What are you waiting for?" she called to him. Her words were muffled through the glass. "Let's go!"

He took a deep breath and obeyed. It'd be fine, he told himself. Having feelings for Lexie didn't change anything. He stepped out of the truck and shut the door, then stilled as Lexie went up on her toes and kissed his cheek for the second time in a week.

"Thank you for bringing me here. This is going to be amazing." She lifted her bag from the truck and went to meet the others, leaving him standing there wondering how he'd ever survive the next few days.

Lexie breathed in the fresh air, crisper than the air anywhere else on earth. At least that's the way it felt. This was the prescription she needed to be giving everyone who walked into her office: clean, fresh air out in nature. She was pretty pleased with the prescription she'd given Clara, too. Instead of a bottle, they were trying exercise and diet first. There was nothing wrong with blood pressure pills, and Clara might ultimately have to take a real prescription. It felt good to try the natural method first, though, under her and Dr. Marcus's guidance.

"The kids seem to be doing a good job," she said as Mason walked up. She'd helped unload a lot of the equipment and was resting under his orders. "I'm impressed at their tent-pitching skills. I thought kids these days only knew their way around a video game."

Mason took a seat beside her. "Wait till you see us make a campfire later."

She looked at the sky where the sun was at its highest point. "This is definitely not what I imagined for myself this summer."

"I'm sorry," he said.

"Not me. As long as no bears come along," she added, halfway serious.

"Can't make any promises there. I'll do my best to rescue you if that does happen, though."

"You always do." She hugged her arms around her body, noticing Amber standing on the outskirts of the crowd. "I think Amber and I will go collect sticks for that campfire you're building later."

He followed her gaze and nodded. "Don't stray too far away from the group. Do you have your phone?"

"So protective," she teased, flashing her cell phone in her pocket. "We'll be back." She approached the girl and waved. "Hey. Want to come help me collect wood for the campfire?"

Amber glanced around and shrugged. "Sure."

They entered into the woods. Lexie made sure to keep her eye on the group as they walked, collecting the sticks with the largest diameter. Amber on the other hand seemed to prefer the thin, brittle sticks. She was slow, bending and straightening as she gathered her sticks. Lexie observed her with concern. Amber was a young girl, and this was a relatively easy task.

"I'm really glad you decided to come along with us," Lexie said after a moment. "So where have you been staying these days?"

Amber startled at the question. She straightened and her eyes widened just a little. But there was nowhere for her to run this time. "I told you that I live with my uncle outside of town."

"But that's not true." Lexie faced her, holding tightly to her armful of wood. "You were staying at my rental home. At least for a few days. If you had somewhere to go, you wouldn't have felt the need to break into my home."

Amber's posture tensed. "I didn't know it was yours. I didn't take anything. I promise."

"I'm not mad. I told you that. I'm just concerned," Lexie said softly.

"I'm eighteen," Amber said for the millionth time. "I don't have to live with family anymore if I don't want to."

Lexie let a moment pass between them. "I just hope you know that if you need help, or a place to crash, I'm here. You can come to me anytime for anything."

Amber lifted her chin. "I heard you're leaving Carolina Shores."

"That's true. I'm returning to my home in Raleigh at the end of the summer. The offer will stand there, too, though. It's only two hours away. You can come stay with me if you need to. I'll come get you."

"Thanks," Amber finally said. "Maybe I will."

Lexie stooped to pick up another stick, trying to keep the conversation casual. "I know you say you're eighteen, but where are your parents?"

The girl looked at the wood in her arms. "This is all I can carry. I'm going to take it back to camp."

"I'll go with you," Lexie said. "We should never be alone, remember?" She meant that for the campsite, and for life in general. If Amber had family, why couldn't she call on them for help?

"Looks good," Dave said, helping them with their wood as they returned to the campsite.

Mason agreed. "I didn't hear you guys screaming, so I'm assuming you didn't run into any wildlife."

"Not on that trip." Lexie smiled even though there was an ache in her spirit for Amber. She couldn't help smiling around Mason, though. His presence made her feel good; her quickened heartbeat when she was near him energized her.

The other kids gathered around.

"Hey Amber," one of the girls, Elaina, said. "We're going on a nature walk. Want to come with us?"

Amber hesitated, then looked at Lexie. "Sure. That sounds great."

Lexie guessed Amber had agreed more to get away from any more questions than to build friendships.

When the girls were gone, Lexie sat in one of the fold-out chairs and sighed.

"Did she open up?" Mason asked, taking a seat directly on the ground beside her. He propped his elbows on his knees.

"No. She's still insisting that she's eighteen, a legal adult. She says she lives with her uncle outside of town, but you and I both know she doesn't. She's lying to us. Not because she's deviant, but because she's scared. I can see it in her eyes."

"We have time," Mason said.

"Two days." Lexie leaned over her knees.

"The thing about nature is that time slows down out here. Two days is a long time." He grabbed a stick and started digging absently in the dirt. "By the time we leave here this weekend, we'll all be lifelong friends."

He glanced up at her, stealing her breath. She wouldn't mind having him as a lifelong friend.

"I'm sure Amber will feel a lot more comfortable around us after the next forty-eight hours," he said.

"Camping does wonders for people. It's therapeutic in a way."

"Did you ever go camping with your wife?" she asked. She didn't know why she wanted to know. The question was too personal and none of her business.

Mason laid his stick down and focused on the tree line in front of him. "Kristin wasn't much of a camper. She liked bike rides and roasting marshmallows by the fire, but that's about it."

"You don't mind talking about her," Lexie observed.

"Why would I? I loved her. I miss her."

"Will you ever—" The words caught in her throat. She didn't need to know the answer to the next question because it didn't affect her. It couldn't affect her.

Mason met her gaze, his blue eyes softening. "I always said I wouldn't," he answered without her finishing her question. "People from church, Clara, everyone's tried to get me to start dating again. It just doesn't feel right."

Lexie nodded, silently reprimanding herself for feeling disappointed by his answer.

"I'm surprised at how easy it was to spend time with you the other night. It was almost like a date."

She swallowed thickly. "Almost," she agreed.

"And it didn't terrify me."

Her heart beat in triple time as she watched and listened to him. "That's amazing because my cooking was pretty terrifying." A soft laugh rumbled through her. What was she doing? She was leaving Carolina Shores in a few short weeks. Starting something she couldn't possibly finish wasn't the best idea.

"What are you two talking about so seriously?" Dave asked, walking up with Jason, another of the adult chaperones.

"Conquering our fears," Mason said, holding her gaze

for just a half second longer. She wouldn't be afraid to jump back into a relationship after Todd. The experience hadn't traumatized her like her mother and friends thought it might. Being left at the proverbial altar just made her see that she needed to listen to her heart more, and seek God's guidance for her life.

She would be afraid to date someone like Mason, though. She didn't want to hurt him. He'd already lost so much, and she couldn't promise him anything.

"There's a swimming hole nearby. I thought we'd take the kids swimming when they get back from their walk," Dave continued, oblivious to her inner turmoil. "Do you know how to swim, Lexie?"

"Like a fish. Sounds perfect." She stood, needing to take a walk herself. "I'll just be over there, scaring off wildlife. Call me when you're ready."

"There's a strict buddy system here," Dave reminded her as she started to walk away. "No one goes anywhere alone, not even the adults." Dave slapped a hand on Mason's back. "You don't mind walking with Lexie, do you, bud?"

If Lexie wasn't mistaken, Dave seemed to be enjoying his reminder of camp rules just a little too much.

Mason stood and headed in her direction. "I told you the people in my life like matchmaking," he said as he closed the distance.

Lexie shrugged. "It just means they care about you. They want you to be happy."

"Right." They headed down one of the dirt paths, through the woods. "I'm sure your friends and family back home want the same for you."

Lexie stooped to pick up a rock, rolling it between her fingers. "I don't see why someone has to be a part of a couple to be happy. I'm happier now without Todd. You can be alone and be happy."

"You can also be with someone and be happy," Mason countered. "It just has to be the right person."

She looked at him, suddenly seeing the right person. At the wrong place and the wrong time.

Chapter Twelve

After a full day of nature walks and swimming, the group settled around a campfire with metal hangers and a bag of marshmallows. The adults had taken extra precaution to be safe with the small fire, emphasizing to the kids the importance of being responsible with matches.

After their walk together, Mason noticed that Lexie had been quiet most of the afternoon.

"Hey." She sat beside him now with her metal hanger and poked a marshmallow on the end. "I haven't done this since I was a child."

"My grandfather used to do this with my brother and me in his fireplace." Mason grimaced. "Not exactly a shining example of fire safety."

She gave him a questioning look.

"My brother caught his marshmallow on fire one time and tossed the hanger on my grandmother's brand-new carpet. I've never seen that woman so angry." He laughed at the memory.

"Is that why you decided to become a fireman?" Lexie asked, joining him as he laughed. "To save all Carolina Shores' residents from the same fate?"

"No." Mason gave his head a hard shake. "My dad

was a fireman. He's retired. He and my mom live in Florida now." He glanced over. "They heard that all retirees move to Florida."

Lexie laughed again and his heart soared. He wanted to make her laugh again and again.

"I like Carolina Shores too much to ever leave," he said. "It's my home. Always will be, I guess."

"I can see why you love it."

He gestured at her marshmallow. "I think you, uh…"

"Oh, no!" She followed his gaze to the burned marshmallow on the end of her hanger.

"You held it over the fire too long. There's an art to roasting marshmallows, you know?"

"Evidently," she agreed, suspending her hanger away from the fire. She tried to remove the blackened treat, but drew her hand back. "Ouch!"

"Here. Let me." Mason took her hanger from her and knocked the marshmallow off. Replacing it with a new one, he did the honors of holding it to the fire. "We won't get distracted this time." A moment later, he presented her with a golden-brown marshmallow. "Best to eat it while it's hot," he said.

She tapped her fingers along the marshmallow to make sure she didn't burn herself, then pulled it off the hanger and took a bite. "Very good," she hummed.

"As good as my chili?" he asked, teasing her.

"And my uncooked chicken." She chuckled, licking the stickiness off her fingers. "You and I might need to invest in culinary classes."

"I hear that Clara is teaching you a thing or two. Maybe we can learn together."

"Clara would love that." She redirected her attention to the teens. "Amber seems to be getting along well with the other kids," Lexie said, tipping her head discretely at the other side of the fire.

Mason nodded. "Maybe I'll take a chance and try to talk to her tonight."

"Hopefully she'll open up."

An hour later, everyone lay in their sleeping bags, staring at the stars. The kids were entertaining themselves by trying to decipher various astrological formations. Better that than playing video games, Mason decided, glancing over at Lexie to make sure she was okay. She was lying beside the girls in the group. He watched her point to a star excitedly, and his heart kicked a little.

"You're falling for her," Dave said, lying next to him.

Mason looked over. He considered pretending not to know what his friend was talking about, but decided to be honest with Dave. And himself. "A little. Yeah."

"That's great, buddy. It's time." Dave propped himself up on an elbow and rolled toward him. "She's great."

"Yeah. But she's also temporary."

"Is that the only thing keeping you from taking a shot with her?" Dave asked.

Mason sighed, focusing on the dark sky above him. "Yeah," he finally said, surprising himself.

"Think of it like dipping your toes in the water before you dive in."

Mason grinned at the analogy. He hadn't done that today at the swimming hole. He'd just dived into the lake. "Dating Lexie would be dipping my toes in the water?" he clarified.

Dave nodded. "Exactly. You don't have to marry her."

Mason took that advice in. He'd never been the type of guy who dated just for the sake of dating. He'd married his high school sweetheart. Dating was for the purpose of determining if the relationship was for forever. If it wasn't, he wasn't interested.

Which was why dating Lexie was out of the question. She wasn't staying in Carolina Shores forever, and he was. And he wasn't sure he'd ever be ready for marriage again.

"You don't have to have all the answers, buddy. If she turns out to be 'the one,' God will work it out for you."

Mason turned to him. "I already met 'the one.'"

Dave frowned. "No one said it can't happen twice for you. 'The one' doesn't mean the one and only person you'll ever fall in love with. 'The one' means the one person who makes you feel like you can do anything. The one person who takes your breath away, and who you can't breathe without."

Mason's chest tightened. "Never pegged you as a romantic."

"Never pegged you as a chicken," Dave countered, punching his shoulder lightly. Then he lay back and they looked at the stars together until they fell asleep.

Lexie illuminated her steps with the flashlight app on her cell phone. She'd awoken in the middle of the night to use the bathroom. There were no bathrooms in the woods, though. At least not the kind she preferred. Not wanting to disturb the group, she'd bypassed the buddy rule only for a few minutes and was now making her way back to camp.

The noises of the night seemed to be louder as she hurried. Each twig she stepped on snapped loudly beneath her feet. Then with a thud, she stubbed her toe on a rock, dropped her cell phone, and *oomph!* She hit the damp ground in front of her.

"You all right?" a deep voice asked, approaching from the front.

Lexie covered her mouth before she screamed, surprised that anyone else was awake. She saw the dark outline of a man coming toward her.

"Shh. Just me," Mason said, reaching for her phone and inspecting it. "It's not broken. Are you okay?"

Swallowing, she took note of her body. Her knee stung. "I think I scraped my knee in the fall. And I banged my toe on that rock back there."

"Didn't you listen to the rule about not leaving the group?" he asked, crouching beside her.

"I didn't want to wake anyone. Did I wake you?" she asked.

"No. I was already awake. I saw you leave and waited a reasonable amount of time before coming after you."

She was thankful for that fact. "Couldn't sleep?" she asked.

"Something like that." He stood. "I know where that first aid kit you made us is. I'll be right back."

"You're leaving me?" she asked, her voice rising slightly.

In the light coming off his own phone, she saw his eyebrows lift. "Now you're scared? You came out here alone. I'll be right back. I don't want to wake the others. I'll help you get cleaned up and then we'll go back to sleep."

She hesitated, then nodded her agreement. "But hurry. I'm a sitting duck for all the night creatures. But don't hurry too much because I don't want you to fall, too."

Mason laughed. "I'd have the first aid kit and be back by now if you'd stopped talking and let me go."

She blew out a breath. "Okay. Go." She watched him walk away, counting the seconds until he returned.

A moment later he held up the white plastic kit. Lexie

pointed to the items in her medical bag, instructing him on what to do as they sat together alone. Having a buddy everywhere you went was a good idea, but right now it felt wrong to be by herself with Mason in the dark. Her heart raced each time he looked at her.

What am I? A teenage girl again? Lexie thought, reprimanding herself. So he was a good-looking guy. So what? So his eyes made her feel like she was falling into this bottomless hole that she never wanted to escape from. That didn't mean she was having real feelings for him.

Mason looked up from what he was doing and smiled. Lexie melted into the log she was seated on. He patted the bandage lightly. "All done."

She looked down at her knee, where a tan-colored Band-Aid was now secured. "Already? That was fast."

He lifted a shoulder, still flashing his pearly teeth in the dark. "We get first aid training at the station. Nearly every few months."

She nodded. "You're a doctor in your own right, then."

He breathed a laugh. "I don't think I could ever do what you do. I'm an adrenaline junkie. I like to rush into danger."

"And I like to run from it." She saw the argument rising in his expression and nodded before he could remind her that she'd done exactly the opposite on the first day they met. And again just now when she'd entered the woods alone. "Maybe we have more in common than we think."

"I think you're right," he said.

Lexie realized her leg was still in Mason's hand. She pulled it away, lowering it to the ground. Her eyes met his for a dangerous second. He didn't look away. Neither did she. And for a moment it crossed her mind that he might kiss her, and she might let him.

Her heart raced in her chest.

"We better get back to the group," he finally said, but his gaze didn't shift.

"Right."

He ran a hand through his hair. Then he stood and helped pull her up. He held on to her until she was steady on her legs. "I'll, uh, see you in the morning, Lexie."

A heat moved over her. Part embarrassment, part complete and utter love of the way her name sounded on his lips.

They walked back to camp and then she disappeared into her sleeping bag, doubting she'd get any more shut-eye tonight.

Mason cracked an eye and groaned at the beating sun. He sat up, never one to just lie around and wait for his body to wake up. He was surprised that he'd actually fallen asleep at all last night. He glanced around, did a quick headcount of the boys, and then walked over to check on the girls, all of whom were sleeping. Except Amber.

"Good morning," he said. "Have you been up long?"

"An hour." She shaded her eyes with her hand. "I made coffee." She gestured to the camping coffeemaker—Lexie's one condition on saying yes to the trip.

"Another reason I'm glad you came with us. Care to join me for a cup?" he asked, praying she'd agree.

Amber stood up. "I don't drink coffee, but I'll come along."

Mason grabbed a mug and poured himself a healthy serving, becoming more alert just by inhaling the aroma. He was loving every minute out here in nature, but he did miss Clara's morning coffee, which was just the right strength. "Sleep well?" he asked, taking a long sip.

"Until Ms. Lexie screamed and woke me up." Amber grinned. It was nice to see an unguarded emotion from her.

"You heard that, huh?"

"I'm surprised that no one else did. Also, she talks in her sleep."

Mason cocked an eyebrow. "What does she say?"

Amber shrugged. "Doctor stuff. I couldn't really make any of it out."

Mason chuckled. "I'm sorry your sleep was disturbed."

"It's okay. I'm used to it. I have a baby sister at home."

Mason looked at her. "Oh, yeah?"

Amber looked down at her hands in her lap. "She cries all the time. Sometimes I get up with her."

He took a breath before responding. It felt like he was in a burning house and each step threatened to bring everything crashing down around him. "I'm sure she misses you."

Amber was quiet. So quiet he started to think she wasn't going to say anything else. "I miss her, too." She sniffed, and then swiped a hand under her nose.

"When was the last time you saw her?" Mason continued to sip from his coffee, watching the sun slowly begin to rise in the sky. From the corner of his eye, he saw other campers begin to stir, too. He prayed they wouldn't walk over just yet, not before Amber had said all she wanted to say, needed to say.

"A month." Amber picked at her nails. "I'm really sorry about breaking into Ms. Lexie's home. I only stayed there a couple of nights."

"Why? Did something happen where you were?"

She continued to pick. "Have you ever done anything you regretted?"

Mason considered her question. "We all have regrets, I guess. No one's perfect."

"You don't understand." She shook her head, keeping it down.

"Try me."

Glancing up at him, she looked younger than the eighteen years she claimed to be. He could tell her trust was teetering. He could also see how much she wanted to tell somebody what was bothering her.

"How about I tell you something I've done?" he asked.

Amber lifted a shoulder. "You've done something you regret?"

Mason interlocked his fingers in his lap. "I used to be married. Did you know that?"

Amber nodded. "I've seen the picture at the Teen Center. She was really pretty."

"Yeah. She was. And nice and smart. The best woman I've ever known. She made me fall in love with her. Then she died." The old familiar pain came rushing through him. "The last time I saw her before the accident…" He hesitated. He'd never talked to anyone about this. Not Dave or Clara. Not even his pastor. He was so ashamed. But if he could help Amber, he would. "The last time I saw her, I yelled at her."

Mason glanced over, waiting to see the look of reproach on Amber's face. He didn't. "I had a stressful day at work, which is no excuse. We never fought. That was the one and only time I ever yelled at her. And it was one of the last things I ever said to her. She got in a car accident on the way to the grocery store that afternoon."

Sure, he and Kristin had talked at the scene of the accident and on the way home after she'd been prematurely discharged from the hospital, but the air was still tense around them. He'd needed to apologize, but he was stubborn.

Amber reached out and touched his forearm. "I'm sorry."

"Me, too. Kristin didn't hold grudges, though. I know in my heart that she would've forgiven me. I just don't get to tell her I'm sorry. I regret that. A whole lot."

Amber folded her legs underneath her. "Thanks for telling me your story."

He sniffed, surprised at how much better he felt. It was true, talking things through did make you feel better. He hoped that if Amber told him what was bothering her, she'd feel better, too. "So," he said, clearing his throat, preparing to ask Amber if she wanted to talk about what was keeping her away from home. Before he could say anything else, however, another of the teens walked up.

"Can I have a cup, too?" Trevor asked.

Mason looked him over. "It'll stunt your growth. Thought you wanted to play pro basketball one day."

"That's not true that coffee stunts growth," Trevor said, crossing his arms. He looked back at Lexie, who was on her way toward them. "Dr. Lexie, will coffee really stunt my growth?"

Lexie shared a look with Mason. "A glass of milk would be better. But since we're out here, you'll have to make do with water."

Trevor frowned. "That's unfair. Are you going to tell me I can't have one of those doughnuts in the cooler, too?"

"That you can have," Mason said, leaning over and lifting the cooler's lid. "But just one."

"Yes!" Trevor lifted a doughnut and went to sit with some others.

Amber slipped away, too, before Mason could ask her any more questions. Lexie sat in her place.

"I was so close to getting something out of her." He finished off his coffee and poured himself another cup, also pouring coffee into Lexie's mug. "Sleep okay?" he asked.

"I did."

"No dreams of doctor stuff?" he asked, remembering what Amber had told him about Lexie talking in her sleep.

Lexie's brows furrowed. "No. I don't think so."

He laughed. "You want a doughnut, too."

"I'd love one." She held open her hand and took the doughnut he offered. "So what's on the agenda today?" she asked.

"Fishing for our dinner. You game?"

She licked a smudge of chocolate off her finger. "I am always ready for a new adventure."

"One thing I like about you," he said. *One of many.*

Lexie had been sitting for over an hour, trying, and failing, to catch a fish. This was harder than it looked. Especially when there were three teenage girls beside her, giggling.

"Mason said we'll never catch anything if we aren't quiet," Lexie warned. "Then what will we eat for dinner?"

The girls stopped talking momentarily to look at her.

"You didn't bring extra food just in case?" Elaina asked.

Lexie shrugged a shoulder. "That's cheating. We're supposed to be doing this right. Real camping."

The girls didn't seem as excited.

"How about this?" Lexie looked at her watch. "Ten

minutes. I'll time it. We'll all stay quiet for ten minutes and see if the fish start biting."

The three girls looked at each other and then nodded.

Lexie thought it might actually be a small feat if they made it that long, but she'd give them the benefit of the doubt. Pressing a button on her watch, she nodded to them that the countdown had started. With their lines dropped into the water, they all sat like little statues on the lakeside.

Mason was right. Time was slower out here. One minute felt like five. Lexie stared at her bobber, willing it to dunk. Then she lifted her gaze and looked at Mason across the lake. The guys had decided sitting next to the girls while fishing was a hopeless cause. Lexie had taken offense initially, but now she understood. It was slightly harder on this side of the lake, but things were about to change.

Lexie looked at her motionless bobber again. Looked at her watch. She waited. Nothing. Then a flicker of excitement came from the other side of the lake, where Mason was reeling in a fish. Not just any fish—a monstrous fish that the other guys were practically jumping up and down over.

Amber and the others looked at Lexie, who sighed.

"It's been nine minutes. I guess we'll end our silence."

"No way," Amber said. "We can't let the guys outdo us like that. We'll be quiet as long as it takes."

The other girls nodded their agreement.

Lexie was proud of their determination. She admired it. "Okay," she said. "Let's catch some fish!"

By the time they headed back to camp, the girls had caught nearly eight fish, none of them as large as the one Mason had caught, but it was a respectable load.

"Anyone know how to clean these things?" Lexie

asked, leaning over the bucket. Where was Clara when she needed her?

"You've been to medical school. Don't tell me you can't skin a few scales." Mason turned an empty bucket over and sat on it.

Lexie started to argue with him until she realized he was joking.

"I'll do it," he said then. "I don't mind."

She relaxed a little. She really hadn't wanted to do the job. "Thanks."

"How'd you get the girls to be quiet long enough to lure any of these guys to your side of the lake anyway?"

"Nope. I'm not telling my secrets. If I do you won't need me next year."

"Next year, huh?" Mason gazed out on the kids enjoying a game of Frisbee a few yards away.

"This is the Teen Center's first annual camping trip, right? You'll have another?" Lexie asked.

He rubbed his chin. "I hadn't thought that far ahead. But it would be nice. This is going well so far. The kids are enjoying themselves." He looked at her. "You'd come back to Carolina Shores just for this?"

Her mouth went dry as he looked at her. The truth was she'd be coming back for him as much as the Teen Center. "Of course I would. I hold the secret to keeping the girls quiet long enough to catch fish. You need me."

"We do need you," he said, a serious tone in his voice. "We couldn't have done this weekend without you, Lexie. Really."

She shrugged. "Okay. Fine. I'll help you clean these fish if you'll teach me."

Mason's mouth fell open. "You never cease to amaze me, Dr. Lexie Campbell. I give you an out with the dirty work and you decide you want to do it anyway. You're one tough cookie."

"I thought you knew that about me." She laughed, dipping to pull out the first fish from the bucket. It flopped in her hand and she squealed, nearly letting it loose.

"You've got to hold it tighter than that," Mason said, wrapping his hand over hers.

Her breathing and her heart stopped with his touch.

"Hold it like this." Mason adjusted her hand and held hers tightly.

She swallowed. "Got it." When he let go, she resisted pulling him back toward her. Having his arms wrapped around her had felt right, even if he was just helping her hold on to a floppy fish. She'd felt safe and content wrapped in his arms. Then he handed her a knife. She felt the blood drain from her face. "I save lives. I don't take them."

He stared at her, dumbfounded. "You said you wanted to help."

Lexie looked at the floppy fish, fighting for its life. "We always threw the fish back when I was a child."

Trevor joined them. "We did, too. The one and only time my father took me fishing."

Amber paled as she looked at the would-be dinner.

"You guys are kidding, right? You want me to toss them back? What'll we eat?"

"There's some peanut butter and jelly," Lexie suggested. "And a loaf of bread."

Without any more protest, Mason lifted the bucket of fish and started walking back to the lake to set what would've been his seafood dinner free.

Mason woke before the sun had started to rise. Among a group of teenagers, he'd have expected he'd be the only one up. He wasn't, though. For the second morning in a row, Amber was already awake, sitting away from the others. And if he wasn't mistaken, she had her head bowed and she was praying.

That was something else he didn't know about her.

He waited for her to lift her head before approaching her and sitting down. "Hey."

She offered a small smile.

"Did Lexie keep you up again last night?"

Amber laughed and shook her head. "No. She was quiet last night."

"Good. I see you made the coffee again. Thank you." He grabbed his mug and poured a serving, breathing in the aroma. After a moment he looked at her. "I saw you praying just now. Do you go to church?"

She looked at him, clearly weighing how much she would disclose.

Please, God, he prayed silently. If she didn't trust him, she'd never tell him anything.

"Every Sunday," she said. "Or I did. I haven't been in a while."

"Why not?" he asked, already knowing. Amber wasn't living at home right now.

"Um…" She twisted her mouth to one side. Her face was growing pale, Mason noticed.

"You all right?"

"Just feeling kind of sick," she said, reaching for a bag of bread nearby. Pulling out a slice, she took a bite. Her hands shook slightly as she held it.

"You can trust me, Amber. I don't know what's going on with you, but I can help. If you let me."

She looked at him with hesitation.

Please, God, Mason prayed again, desperately wanting to help the girl beside him.

"I'm pregnant," she finally said, taking another bite.

Mason's eyes widened. Of all the things he'd thought she might say, he hadn't expected that.

"My father is a pastor." Chewing, she looked over at him. Her eyes were glassy, large and scared.

"You think he won't love you anymore?" Mason asked.

Amber shook her head. "No. My mother and father will always love me. I know that."

"Then why did you leave home?" Mason asked gently. "Did you tell them?"

She shook her head again. "I don't want to disappoint them. If they knew, they'd be so disappointed in me. *I* am so disappointed in me. I never meant to…" She shook her head as a tear escaped down her cheek. Her chest shuddered as she took a deep breath and chewed her bite of bread.

"Don't you think they're concerned about you right now? How will you take care of a baby living in abandoned houses?"

Amber took another bite of bread, the pallor of her face slowly turning rosy again. "I'm not. I'm not planning on staying away from home forever. Or I wasn't. The longer I stay away, though, the harder it is to go back. I don't know what to do." Her body seemed to crumple as she started to cry. "I'm just so, so sorry."

Mason glanced down at her flat stomach. She wasn't showing yet, but he doubted she'd been getting the nutrition she needed for herself and a growing baby. He wrapped an arm around her. "Shh. It's okay. It's going to be okay," he said, holding her for a long moment. Then she pulled away and he looked at her seriously. "When you become a parent your priorities change. Your decisions have to be made with what's best for the child in mind," he told her.

Amber looked over. "I'm going to be a good mother."

"I know you will. But that child needs to be monitored by a doctor. So do you. The baby needs good nutrition and a mother who's safe. And it sounds to me like he or she is going to have some awesome grandparents. Your baby needs them."

More tears streamed down Amber's cheeks.

"You need your parents right now, too. You can't do this alone." He turned as Lexie walked up behind him. Her look of concern moved from him to Amber.

"Will you take me home?" Amber asked in a small voice. "I'm ready to go home."

Mason wrapped the girl in his arms and held on to her tight, looking up at Lexie and offering a small smile. "I'd be happy to."

Chapter Thirteen

Amber, whose real name was Emily Simpson, was quiet as she rode in the back cab of Mason's truck. Lexie could almost feel the anxiety radiating off her. She'd be fine, though. She'd assured them that she hadn't run because of anything her parents had done. She'd run because she was ashamed and didn't know how to tell them that she was pregnant. Emily had gone through a period of rebellion and had done a lot of things her parents hadn't approved of. But she'd learned the hard way that their rules and boundaries were meant to keep her safe.

Lexie had also learned that Emily's parents had filled out a missing persons report, but the descriptions hadn't matched. Despite being two months pregnant, Emily was thinner now. She was also taller than what her parents had reported and her hair had been lightened by the sun this summer.

"I want you to make a prenatal appointment first thing on Monday morning," Lexie said, turning to glance into the back seat. "You need to start taking prenatal vitamins, too. We have some at the health clinic if you want to stop by."

Emily nodded. "Okay."

In the back seat of the car, she looked like a scared little girl—still a child in her own right.

"Can you be my doctor?" Emily asked, hugging her arms around her body.

"No, honey. I'm not trained in obstetrics. I'm a general practitioner." Lexie returned to facing forward.

"Maybe Dr. Marcus can recommend a good one, though," Mason suggested.

Lexie nodded. "I'm sure he can. I'll call him when we get home."

Mason turned into a quaint neighborhood just outside of Carolina Shores, slowing his truck as he approached the cul-de-sac where Emily lived. "We'll be keeping in touch. And you know how to find Lexie and me if you ever need us," he said, glancing over his shoulder.

Emily nodded.

"And don't forget about the Teen Center. Don't be a stranger with us. You've made quite a few friends. You'll need your friends and family now, more than ever."

Emily's breath was audible from the back seat. Even though she'd already spoken to her father on the phone and told him she was on her way home, she looked terrified. "Thank you for everything."

Lexie met her gaze and offered a warm smile. "It's going to be okay. I promise." She couldn't guarantee that Emily's parents wouldn't still be upset after the relief of having her home. They might even refuse to help her, but Lexie doubted it. She'd spoken to Emily's father, too, assuring him that his daughter was in good hands right now. Her father had seemed genuinely concerned.

Mason stopped in front of a brick-style ranch house. Emily's parents were already waiting on the front porch as he pulled in.

Lexie's heart kicked as she watched the girl take off

running toward them. Her father opened his arms wide, embracing her. "I think she's going to be fine," Lexie said with tears in her eyes.

Mason nodded. He had tears in his eyes, too, she noticed. "This weekend was an all-around success." He waved at Emily and her parents, then started driving again. "Thanks for coming with us."

"Thanks for inviting me." Lexie hugged her arms around her body. "It feels strange going home after a weekend of camping. You're right. Time slowed down out there. Feels like we've been away forever."

He grinned at her.

"What?" she asked, swiping at a loose strand of hair on her cheek.

"You just referred to Carolina Shores as home. Looks like we're growing on you."

"I like the scenery. And the people are fantastic," she said, teasing him.

They drove in silence for a few more minutes, and then Mason cleared his throat. "So earlier in the week I told you that instead of you cooking for me, or me cooking for you, that I'd take you out to eat. To a restaurant."

Lexie's heart sped up. "I remember."

"Some might call that a date," he said, looking over.

"Some might," she agreed. "Or it might just be two friends having a meal."

Mason shook his head. "I like you as more than a friend, Lexie."

She forced herself to take a deep breath. "I like you as more than a friend, too." *A lot* more.

"So what do you say? Can I take you out sometime? On a date? Maybe next weekend? Let's see if we have something worth investigating between us."

She hesitated.

He held up a hand. "I know you're not staying in Carolina Shores. I know you're leaving in a few weeks."

"Then what's the point?" she asked honestly, even though she wanted to say yes so badly the word ached in her throat. She'd been fantasizing about Mason asking her on a real date. Seeing his face had started to become the highlight of her day; spending time with him was something she looked forward to like a child anticipating their birthday or a plate of dessert. She felt giddy at the thought of him, something she hadn't experienced in a very long time.

"I'm not sure. All I know is I want to spend more time with you. If that continues to be true, we'll find a way to make it happen, no matter where we are."

Lexie nodded. "Then I say yes," she finally said. "I'd love to go on a date with you." It already felt like they'd been on several dates anyway. They'd spent most of their free time together so far this summer, getting to know each other. And the more she got to know Mason Benfield, the more she liked him.

"Good. I'll look forward to it."

She pulled her lower lip between her teeth, trying not to do a happy dance of excitement in his passenger seat. "Me, too."

Half an hour later, he pulled into the driveway of her rental home and helped her unload her bags.

"Tell Clara hello for me," Lexie called as he walked back to his truck and got in. "Tell her I'll come see her tomorrow afternoon for our daily walk." She'd missed the past few days walking with Clara. Hopefully she had kept up with her exercise routine on her own. And her healthy eating plan, too.

"I'll tell her." Mason waved and started backing his truck out of the driveway.

It felt good to be home, she thought, catching herself thinking of this place as home again. Not the rental home, but the town and the people. *Mason.*

Her phone buzzed, signaling a voice mail. She hadn't even heard it ring, but she'd been preoccupied by her handsome driver on the ride here. She clicked a button and held her phone to her ear, listening to the voice on the other line.

"Good morning, Dr. Campbell. This is Dr. Stevens from Raleigh Medical. We're calling to formally invite you to come interview with us for a position as one of our staff physicians. I've heard so many good things about you. Please give me a call back when you can." The doctor left a return phone number, and the message ended.

Lexie hung up and sighed. She should've been jumping up and down about the message. Her parents had led her to believe that this job was all but hers. All she needed to do was go through the formalities of interviewing for it. She stared at her phone, not feeling even an inkling of joy over the invitation. Maybe she didn't want the job anymore. Maybe she was starting to consider Dr. Marcus's offer for the health clinic. He'd told her there was a full-time position there for her, too. It wasn't as prestigious according to some, but the reason she'd always wanted to become a doctor was to help people who were sick and hurting. She was doing that here in Carolina Shores.

Lexie set her phone on the coffee table. The message could wait. She needed more time to think about her decision.

Mason felt lighter than air. Amber, aka Emily, was finally home and safe, and he had a date with Lexie scheduled for next weekend.

He dialed Dave's phone number as he drove.

"Hey," Dave answered. Mason could hear the wind in the background. Dave was driving with the windows down. "Did you get Amber home all right?" he asked.

"Yep. Her real name is Emily Simpson. I think she's going to be just fine. How about you guys? Did everyone get all packed up without difficulty?" Mason and Lexie had left early to go ahead and take Emily home. Once she'd decided it was time, they hadn't wanted to give her a chance to change her mind, back out, or run away again. She was eighteen, legally an adult according to the law. But she was still a scared kid in his eyes who needed her parents, especially now. She had a child on the way, and she'd felt like she was all alone. There'd been a time in his life when he had felt the same way. Like he'd been all alone in the world. It hadn't been true, of course. He'd always had God. And then Clara had come knocking down his door and brought him to live with her and Rick.

"Depends on what you mean by 'without difficulty,'" Dave said.

Mason could hear the humor interlaced in his friend's voice. "Uh-oh. What happened?"

"Oh, you know. A bear ran off with the rest of our food. We decided to grab some burgers and fries on the way home. The kids considered that a blessing from the Big Guy upstairs."

Mason laughed. Good thing Lexie had left before the bear incident. That might've ruined her for all future camping trips. "I bet they did." He pulled into the Carlyles' driveway and parked. "Glad to hear everyone's okay. I'll talk to you later, buddy."

"You bet."

Shoving his cell phone back into his pocket, Mason

headed toward the side entrance of Clara and Rick's home. He hadn't seen Clara in a few days, and he was certain she'd be upset if he didn't come say hello to her first thing.

"Clara?" he called, wiping his feet on the welcome mat. "Clara, it's Mason. I'm home." He expected to be greeted by the smell of something good cooking in the kitchen. Clara was always cooking up something, and the fact that he'd been gone so long made it more likely she'd have prepared something to welcome him back. She was like that, and he didn't mind it one bit.

There were no yummy smells floating in the air, though, as he entered the house. "Clara?" he called again, as a prickle of worry rode through him.

"In the kitchen," she finally answered. Her voice was smaller than usual.

The alarms in his gut started ringing, and he walked faster. "Hey. You okay?" he asked, finding her sitting in the dark at the kitchen table, holding her head in her hands.

"I'm fine, dear. A little headache is all." She didn't lift her head to look at him, though.

Mason went to the sink and poured her a glass of water. Then he brought it to her. "Have you taken anything for it?"

She started to nod, then winced in pain. "I took two aspirin a few hours ago."

"A few hours ago?" he asked, growing more concerned. "You've had this headache for a few hours?"

Clara tried to nod again, then groaned.

"Where's Rick?" he asked.

"He's fishing, dear. He left his cell phone on the kitchen counter."

Mason glanced back and spotted Rick's phone. A lot

of good it did there. "I think maybe I should take you to the doctor, Clara."

She shook her head quickly, then pressed her eyes shut. "Call Lexie. She'll know what to do."

"No offense, Clara, but Lexie is new at being a doctor. I'd feel a lot better if you saw someone with more experience. If you don't want to go to the emergency room, I'll drive you to the urgent care facility outside of town. Dr. Evans or Dr. Piper will be there."

"No need." Clara started to stand. He knew she didn't like to worry people. "Maybe I'll just go lie back down in my bed." She took a couple of steps, then paused, swaying back and forth on her feet.

Mason grabbed her arm, steadying her. "I'm going to insist on this, Clara. You can send me to bed without dinner later."

As he took her arm, she went weak. Her full body weight fell into him. With strong arms, he hoisted her up and carried her to the truck. He took care of the people he loved, and he loved Clara as much as he did his own family. He needed to make sure this was just an ordinary headache because from where he was standing it didn't appear to be.

Clara stirred in his seat as he drove, making his way to the hospital as fast as he could. The urgent care facility was out of the question now. This was an emergency. "Mason?"

"Shh. Don't try to talk. I'm taking you to the ER. No arguments."

She didn't say a word. A few minutes later, he helped her walk into the small emergency room wing off the side of the main hospital.

A nurse came to her side as she entered. Thankfully, the ER wasn't packed today.

"What's going on?" the nurse asked.

"A bad headache," Mason said. "She said she's had it for a few hours."

"Do you have a history of migraines?" the nurse asked, looking concerned.

Clara shook her head lightly, wincing. "I have high blood pressure, though."

Mason stiffened. That was news to him. "Since when?" he asked as the nurse continued writing in Clara's chart.

"Lexie checked me out last week at the health clinic. She said I had moderately high blood pressure."

Mason's own head was starting to hurt now. "She didn't say anything to me about that."

"We were controlling it with diet and exercise, dear," Clara said, rubbing her temple. "Can I lie down?" she asked the nurse. "I'm really not feeling well."

"Of course." The nurse stepped behind the wheelchair that they'd seated Clara in. She escorted them through a hall into a curtained room and positioned the wheelchair directly beside the bed. Then she pushed a few buttons to lower the bed to the height of the wheelchair's seat.

Clara only had to make a few motions to sit herself on the bed. Lying back, she sighed, and then cracked her eyes to look at Mason. "Will you go find Rick for me? You know where he likes to fish. On the banks of Old Point River."

Mason nodded, unable to bear seeing Clara in so much pain. "Is she going to be okay?" he asked the nurse quietly, hoping that Clara couldn't overhear. She didn't like people to make a fuss over her.

"We'll take good care of her, sir," the nurse said, which wasn't much assurance. He knew as well as anyone that sometimes people walked into a hospital and never walked out. Or they did, but then they didn't make it far. Fresh fear sparked inside him.

What was Lexie thinking treating Clara on her own?

"I want to talk to the doctor on shift before I leave," he said.

"Now, Mason. That's not necessary," Clara said.

"It is. I'm not leaving you until I know you're in good hands." Experienced hands.

The nurse nodded. "I'll page the doctor."

"Thank you." Mason glanced over at Clara. If anything happened to her, he wasn't sure what he would do.

A minute later, an older man in a white lab coat walked in. Mason was relieved to hear that the doctor had decades of treating cases just like Clara's under his belt. He had a plan and a lot of big words.

"I'll go find Rick now," he told Clara after interrogating the doctor. "I won't be gone long."

She nodded, looking weaker than he'd ever seen her.

Stepping out into the hallway, Mason left to go to Old Point River as Clara had asked him to. After that he planned on finding the good Doctor Lexie and exchanging a few words with her.

Lexie awoke with a start. Someone was banging on her front door. Checking her nightstand clock, she saw that it was 9:00 p.m. She'd fallen asleep early, exhausted from the camping trip. She quickly pushed her feet into a pair of slippers and hurried to the front of the house, checking the peephole to see who her visitor was. Seeing the familiar face, excitement swelled inside her chest. What was Mason doing here at this hour?

She opened the door. "Hi," she said, smiling up at him. Her smile fell as she took in his grim expression.

"What's wrong? Did something happen with Amber? I mean Emily."

He shook his head. "No, this isn't about Emily. Clara is in the hospital."

Lexie's hands flew to her mouth. "What happened? Is she okay?"

"She had a headache," he said through a tight jaw. "Apparently, she's been experiencing lots of headaches related to her high blood pressure lately. Do you know anything about that, Lexie?"

His tone of voice was accusatory. So much so that Lexie took a reflexive step backward.

"Yes. I checked Clara's blood pressure a couple weeks ago. I had her come to my office for a full exam." Dread started to build inside her. "And I've been monitoring her blood pressure since then."

"You never mentioned any of this to me," Mason said, standing stiffly in her doorway.

Lexie shook her head. "I can't. You know that. That would be breaking doctor-patient confidentiality. Plus Clara specifically asked me not to say anything. She didn't want to worry you."

"What are you doing making yourself Clara's doctor anyway?" he asked, anger sparking in his voice. "You've barely been a real doctor for a month. You have no business taking on someone with health risks like Clara."

Lexie drew back. "I'm a good doctor." She wanted to defend her decisions and review Clara's medical history with him, but that would be breaking Clara's confidence.

"So good that Clara is lying in a hospital bed at Carolina Medical right now. She could die in there and that would be your fault."

Tears burned behind Lexie's eyes. Why was Mason treating her this way all of a sudden? This wasn't her fault. "Just tell me what happened. Is she okay?" Her voice cracked. Was this really as serious as Mason was making it out to be?

Mason blew out a breath. "She's under the care of more experienced doctors now. They're monitoring her blood pressure, something you never should've been doing."

Lexie crossed her arms under her chest, willing herself not to cry. "Oh, are you a doctor now, too?" she asked, getting defensive. "I tried to put Clara on medication. She didn't want it. She refused it actually."

Mason shook his head, obviously not wanting to hear anything she had to say right now.

"Mason," she said, softening her voice. "Look at me. I love Clara. I would never do anything to hurt her. You know that."

"Not intentionally," he said. "You doctors never intentionally mean to hurt someone."

She didn't like the way he grouped her with every other doctor he'd had a bad experience with. She didn't like the chill in his voice as he spoke to her right now, either. It was void of the warmness and care he'd increasingly shown her over the past few weeks. "Mason," she said, reaching out to touch his arm.

He pulled away. Whatever warmness and care he'd felt for her before was now gone.

Steeling her emotions, she nodded. "I want to go see Clara," she said.

"I think you've done enough." He ran a hand through his hair. "If something happens to Clara, I'm holding you personally responsible."

Lexie trembled as she stood in front of him, fluctuating from anger to hurt to fear that maybe he was right. Maybe she'd done something wrong in her treatment of

Clara. Maybe she'd missed some important symptom. She'd spoken to Dr. Marcus, though. He'd agreed that if Clara preferred to try diet and exercise first, then it was her choice. As long as she knew the risks and possible outcomes. Lexie's treatment of Clara had been sound and she didn't appreciate Mason's accusations otherwise. "You need to leave, Mason, before I say something I'll regret."

She already had a lot of regrets suddenly. If Mason could turn on her so easily, she regretted letting herself fall for him the way she had this summer. Love wasn't quick tempered. It didn't judge. And that's what Mason was doing right now. He was judging her. A relationship was built on a foundation of several things, including trust, and Mason certainly didn't trust her.

"Good night, Lexie," he said, not meeting her eyes.

She didn't respond. Instead, she watched him turn and head back to his truck.

She shut the door behind her and took a breath as tears rolled down her cheeks. When his truck was gone, she grabbed her purse and car keys and walked out to her car. It didn't matter what Mason thought; she was Clara's doctor. She was a good doctor. And right now her patient needed her.

It was dark as Lexie walked through the hospital parking lot and entered the building. She took the elevator, fidgeting with her hands. Clara had to be okay. The diet and exercise was working. They'd been monitoring Clara's condition closely.

A bell rang and the elevator doors opened to the floor that the downstairs receptionist had said Clara was on. Lexie stepped off and headed down the hall to the nurse's station.

"Hi," she said to one of the nurses seated behind a computer. "I'm Dr. Campbell. One of my patients was checked in tonight. I wanted to see how she was doing."

The nurse, a young woman with blond hair that was pulled back into a ponytail, smiled brightly. It never ceased to amaze Lexie how cheerful people who worked in the health care field could be. That was one sign that they were called for the position they were in. They did it joyfully and brought hope to the sick just by being who they were. She'd hoped that she could be that for her patients, too. Now Mason was accusing her of making her patients sicker.

"Patient's name?" the nurse asked.

"Clara Carlyle."

The nurse frowned as she lifted a note on the front of Clara's chart. "Excuse me for just one moment." She got up and went to talk to the charge nurse in the back of the station. A few seconds later the two women approached Lexie together. "Dr. Kellum is now the doctor on Clara Carlyle's case."

Lexie nodded, leaning her elbows on the counter. She'd fully expected another doctor to be caring for Clara while she was in the hospital. That wasn't a problem.

"And we have orders from the family that you are not in any way to care for Mrs. Carlyle or make any decisions regarding her health care. You are no longer on the case," the charge nurse said, looking apologetic.

"The family?" Lexie repeated, her heart splintering into a million little pieces. It was one thing that Mason blamed her, but having Clara and Rick blame her, too, was unbearable. "Okay." She nodded numbly. "Can you just tell me if Mrs. Carlyle is all right?"

The charge nurse smiled gently. "She's resting comfortably."

Lexie nodded. Then she dragged her feet back down the hospital's corridor, through the parking lot to her car and drove home. If she could call it that. Before tonight, she'd started to feel like Carolina Shores was becoming a home to her; now it just felt like one big mistake.

When she was tucked inside her living room, she reached for her cell phone and dialed. The physician in Raleigh who'd wanted to interview her had probably gone home by now, but she wanted to leave him a message. If he was still interested, she'd very much like to interview for the job there, because from her current viewpoint there was no reason to stay in Carolina Shores.

After tossing and turning all night, Mason got up and headed into the house, where Clara would usually be humming cheerily and cooking breakfast. Instead, she was lying in a hospital bed down at Carolina Shores Medical.

"Good morning," Rick said, coming in.

Mason turned. "I thought you'd be at the hospital already."

Rick nodded. "I was. Clara shooed me away. That woman does not like to be taken care of. Takes care of everyone else in her life, but can't stand to be pampered herself."

Mason chuckled softly. "Sounds about right."

"That's one reason she's in that bed right now, you know," Rick said.

"That and the fact that she didn't seek proper medical attention." Mason's jaw tightened again. He didn't want to blame Lexie, but he couldn't seem to help it. She was an amateur. Clara deserved care from an experienced doctor who knew what they were doing.

Rick's brow furrowed. "What do you mean by that? Lexie is a fine doctor. So is Dr. Marcus."

"You knew she was seeing them?" Mason asked.

"Clara mentioned it to me." Rick nodded, pouring himself a cup of coffee. "That's not why she's in the hospital, though. She's there because she overworked herself at the church yesterday. She didn't eat and didn't listen to her body telling her to rest. Simple as that. They're doing more tests this morning to make sure, but that's all it was, son."

Mason crossed his arms. "Lexie said she was monitoring Clara's blood pressure. She and Dr. Marcus didn't even give her medicine to regulate it. You're fine with that?"

Rick shrugged and narrowed his eyes. "I'm no doctor. Far as I know, neither are you."

"Right." Mason nodded. "I'm on my way to see Clara before heading to the fire department."

"Whatever you do, don't make a fuss over that woman," Rick warned on a laugh.

"Wouldn't dream of it."

"If you stop and get her some real food, though, she'll love you forever."

"Noted." Mason headed out the door, trying to make sense of what Rick had just told him. He wanted to change his mind about the situation, but he was stuck. He'd tossed and turned all night thinking about what could've happened to Clara under Lexie's care. He'd also been remembering his last evening with his wife, and thinking about what could've happened if she'd been cared for differently by her first-year physician.

God has a plan in everything. That's what Clara always told him. Mason believed that; he really did. He'd lost Kristin, but he'd gained a passion for what she'd started when she was alive. Half the guys at the firehouse had gained her passion, too. Good things were springing up out of something that had torn his life to shreds.

Mason went through a drive-through to grab Clara's breakfast, then headed to the hospital. He wanted to let go of his anger toward Lexie, but he couldn't. He found safety in the fact that she wouldn't be caring for Clara anymore. He'd specifically asked the charge nurse to make sure of it.

Entering the hospital, he took the elevator up to the third floor. Then he stepped quietly inside Clara's hospital room, careful not to wake her. He set the bag of food on her nightstand, and then jumped as Clara spoke to his back.

"Leaving so soon?" she asked.

He turned and smiled at her. "Good morning, Clara. How are you feeling?"

"Tired of people asking me that question. I'm going home this afternoon, and I can't get there soon enough," she said, spunky as ever.

He laughed, pulling up a chair beside her. He noticed the get-well balloon suspended in the air and Lexie's name scrawled on the gift card. Guilt knotted his stomach.

"It arrived this morning." Clara looked at him with knowing eyes. "And don't you dare try to blame that girl for me getting sick yesterday. I forbid it."

Mason's eyes widened at Clara's harsh tone. He'd rarely heard her raise her voice. "She should've told me what was going on. *You* should've told me what was going on."

Clara frowned. "I didn't want you to worry, which is exactly what you would've done."

"Lexie had a responsibility to—" he started.

Clara held up a hand to quiet him. "Stop right there. Lexie did what I asked her to. Under Dr. Marcus's supervision. If you're looking for an excuse to stay alone, Mason Benfield, don't use me."

He drew back. "I'm not looking for an excuse," he argued. "Why do I need an excuse?"

"You tell me." Clara locked eyes with him, lifting her body off the bed to point a finger into his chest. "You like that girl, and don't you deny it. I have eyes. You two have been flirting all summer, and I'm thrilled as anyone to see it. You deserve to be happy. You deserve to find love again."

"Love?"

She shushed him before he could protest. "But you're scared. That's right. Mason Benfield is one big chicken," she said, her voice rising and her expression challenging him to interrupt her again.

Mason looked behind him, hoping no one was overhearing her lecture. The guys at the fire station would never let him live it down if they heard Clara talking to him this way. "That's not what this is about. My concern for you has nothing to do with how I feel about Lexie. This is about how I feel about you, Clara. I love you, and I don't want to lose you. You could barely stand last night. I've never seen you so weak."

Clara reached for his hand and patted it firmly. "Thank you for caring about me. And I'm sorry for putting you through that, dear."

He squeezed her hand. "Promise me you'll take better care of yourself."

"I promise. But you've got to promise me that you'll think about what I said. About you and Lexie."

He hesitated on his answer. He could deny falling in love with Lexie this summer, but that would be a lie. He'd definitely started to fall for the green-eyed doctor with a heart so big it got her in over her head sometimes. And he'd been there this summer to rescue her when that had happened. He'd been happy to be there for her.

Instead of making any promises to Clara, he lifted the bag of breakfast and dropped it in her lap.

"Is this what I think it is?" she asked, looking up hopefully.

"Rick said you'd love me forever if I got you something other than the cafeteria food here."

"I would've loved you forever anyway." Clara beamed. "That's how love works. Once you're in it, there's no escaping." She winked.

With a nod, he stood and headed to the door. "Rest up. I've got to go to work."

He also had to figure out how to put an end to the feelings he had for Lexie. As usual, Clara was right, even if he didn't want to admit it this time. He was a chicken. Falling for Lexie was terrifying and he'd been looking for a way out since that first skip of his heart in her presence. He wasn't ready to be in love again. And maybe he never would be.

Chapter Fourteen

Lexie held tightly to the smile on her face, refusing to let memories of last night slip into her thoughts. Dr. Stevens had called her back after Mason left and asked if she'd be able to come in for an interview today. Otherwise, he didn't have another availability until the end of next week. Lexie hadn't wanted to wait that long, though.

"Your résumé looks great. I'm impressed by the work you've done at the health clinic in Carolina Shores this summer," Dr. Stevens said. He had a friendly smile, and from what Lexie could tell, he was a nice guy. She'd like working for him. And she'd like working here. The facility was state-of-the-art.

"Thank you. This summer was a great learning experience for me."

"Well, in my opinion, you never stop learning," Dr. Stevens said. "I'm still attending conferences and consulting with physicians on the other side of the world."

Lexie nodded. Dr. Stevens would definitely be a wonderful mentor, even though no one could ever top her admiration for Dr. Marcus.

He closed her file and leaned back in his chair. "I don't

want to waste any time or let anyone else snatch you up. When can you start?"

"Are you offering me the job?" she asked, surprised even though she'd known she had a good shot at getting the position.

"Of course. I think you'd be a wonderful asset to our team."

"Thank you so much."

"Is that a yes?" Dr. Stevens asked.

She wanted to say yes. Really wanted to, in her mind at least. Her heart wasn't feeling it, though. There was no excitement. No joy. Just sadness and disappointment. "Um." She hesitated. "Can I think about it?" she asked.

Dr. Stevens furrowed his brow. "Do you have other interviews lined up? Other offers on the table?" he asked.

"Well…" She thought of what Dr. Marcus had told her. He'd said he'd be happy to have her as a permanent fixture at the health clinic in Carolina Shores. "Just one," she admitted. But she wasn't seriously considering Dr. Marcus's offer, especially after last night. Her summer in Carolina Shores had come to an end and it was time to let go.

Dr. Stevens handed her his business card. "I hope you'll weigh your decisions carefully, Dr. Campbell. We'd love to have you here. Call me when you've had some time to think about it." He patted her shoulder. "Don't think about it too long, though. We do have other interviewees waiting to hear back. None that have impressed me as much as you, though."

"Thank you, sir." As she walked out of the hospital in Raleigh, the breath whooshed out of her. She wished she felt happier about the offer. It was everything she'd ever wanted in a first job. Good hours for a doctor fresh out of medical school, great pay and nice coworkers with mounds of knowledge that she could draw from.

She just needed some time to pray about it. She didn't plan on making any life decisions anymore without ample prayer and time listening to her heart.

Lexie walked through the parking lot and plopped back in her car, feeling the weight of her decision heavy on her chest. Before she could put the key in her ignition, her phone rang inside her purse. She unzipped it and fumbled around, then pulled her cell phone to her ear. "Hello."

"Lexie, dear," Clara's familiar voice said. "Where are you?"

Lexie sucked in a breath. It was good to hear Clara's voice. She'd been hoping that Clara was feeling much better this morning, but after being removed from Clara's care, she'd been hesitant to call and inquire. "Clara. How are you feeling?"

"Much better. My headache is gone and I'm ready to go home. I'm just curious, though, why is my doctor suddenly missing?"

Lexie frowned. "Dr. Kellum hasn't been in to see you?" she asked.

"Dr. Kellum? You're my doctor, dear. Or are you mad at me for overdoing it at the church yesterday?"

Shaking her head, Lexie directed her attention outside the car's window. "I've been removed from your care, Clara. Remember?"

"By whose orders?" Clara asked, her voice rising. "I would never remove you from my care, dear. You're a wonderful doctor and I'm blessed to have you."

"Then who—?" Lexie shook her head as the realization hit her. "Mason. Of course."

Clara hesitated on the other line. "Oh, Lexie. He's just overprotective of me. Don't let this come between you two. You've been growing closer. I've seen it, and it's a wonderful thing."

"Well, a relationship between two people has to have trust. And Mason clearly doesn't trust me." An ache throbbed in Lexie's chest. She'd thought she and Mason had grown closer, too. That they'd surpassed his issues with trust and doctors. She'd thought he'd started to see her as more than that.

Clara groaned on the line. "Oh. I don't want to be the cause of your breakup."

"We were never together," Lexie said reflexively. But she and Mason had been together, in more ways than one. "I'll be back in Carolina Shores to check on you soon," Lexie promised. She still needed to return to her rental home and gather her things. If she intended to return to Raleigh and the job offer she'd just been offered.

"Good."

They said their goodbyes and Lexie placed her phone back in her purse. She paused before putting the key in her ignition. Clara was right. She and Mason had broken up. That made two breakups in one summer. The first one was because she hadn't been listening closely enough to her heart to know that things between her and Todd weren't right. That breakup had been a blessing. She'd thought she was listening to her heart with Mason, though. She'd actually thought that God had led her to Carolina Shores to find him, so that they could find each other. But she'd been wrong.

Cranking the engine, Lexie took a shuddery breath and headed to her parents' home. She'd missed them over the past month. And Grandma Jean. Grandma Jean always had the right words. She'd know what Lexie should do.

Mason had been sitting on the pier and staring out on the calm waters for over an hour. He'd also been praying and hoping that God was doling out answers tonight. He needed to know what to do about his feelings for Lexie. He'd heard from Clara that Lexie was out of town, and he'd gotten the direct impression that was his fault.

Guilt knotted inside him. Demanding that Lexie be removed from Clara's care at the hospital had been harsh. Perhaps he'd overreacted just a little bit. Or a lot. But it was his job to protect the people he loved, wasn't it? If he didn't, who would?

He sighed heavily, knowing what Clara would tell him: God would protect them.

He checked his phone again, wishing without meaning to that Lexie had called. He didn't like how things had been left between them, even if slowing things down, or ending things completely, was probably for the best. She needed to get back to her life in Raleigh and he needed to get back to…life as it'd been before her. The only thing was that his life before her had been empty. He'd been missing something, that spark that Lexie had ignited inside him when she'd broken evacuation barriers at the beginning of the summer. She was fun and joyful, caring and so, so giving of her time, her energy, her love.

He stood and started walking back to his truck. He needed to stop by the Teen Center before going home to check on Clara. She'd been discharged earlier and was adamant that she was okay, which was good news. And the attending physician at the hospital had agreed that Clara's blood pressure was regulated with diet and exercise at the moment. Dr. Marcus would continue to monitor it closely for her. It was a good plan that Lexie had come up with. She was a good doctor and he regretted that he'd suggested otherwise.

A short drive later he walked into the building that hosted his favorite teenagers, one of whom was waiting for him when he arrived.

"Mr. Mason!"

He smiled at Trevor, despite his grumpy mood. "Hey, buddy. What's up?"

"Oh, nothing. Just wanted you to know that I had the best camping trip of my life last weekend."

Mason laughed. "You're the one who told me you'd never been camping before."

"It was still the best. Next year will be even better."

Mason nodded. "I like your enthusiasm." Part of the reason the camping trip had gone so well was because of Lexie. She'd dreamed up a lot of the activities with the kids. She'd kept the mood light and fun. She'd also brought a spiritual element to the trip, ensuring that Bibles were read every night and prayers were offered up at every opportunity.

"So where is Ms. Lexie?" Trevor asked. "Is she coming tonight?"

Mason frowned. "I don't think so, buddy." A heaviness settled around his heart. Even if he'd realized he wasn't ready to start dating again, he did need to find Lexie and apologize at some point. Not just for blaming Clara's illness on her, but for being angry with her and not giving her a chance to speak or explain the situation. He'd been quick to grab onto something, anything, to wedge between them. Because he was afraid of how close they were growing.

"Wanna play basketball with me and Derek?" Trevor asked.

Mason shook his head. "Not just yet. Maybe in a minute or two."

"Which in adult time is an hour." Trevor clucked his tongue. "See you in an hour then, Mr. Mason."

Mason laughed even though he wasn't feeling joy at the moment. He headed to the office, where Dave was sitting behind his desk. "Hey."

"Oh, hey." Dave looked up and frowned. "Word on the street is that you and Lexie broke up."

"What street?" Mason crossed his arms at his chest and leaned against the door frame. "And, for the record, we were never together."

Dave shrugged. "Sure looked like you were to me, but what do I know?" He grabbed his keys and stood. "I'm on shift at the fire station tonight. I told the kids to go easy on you. John will be here in half an hour because I know you're anxious to get back to Clara."

Mason nodded. "Why'd you tell the kids to go easy on me?"

Dave shook his head. "Because Lexie dumped you, of course," he teased.

Mason wasn't amused. "She didn't dump me."

"You dumped her?" Dave turned back as he headed out of the office. "I thought you were smarter than that, buddy."

"No one dumped anyone. We were never together," Mason said again. He had a feeling he'd be getting a lot of questions from people about Lexie. He and Lexie had spent a lot of time together over the past few weeks, and people had started to talk. They weren't gossiping, they were just excited to see him moving on, he suspected.

"I'm just teasing you. Rick brought Clara by earlier. She mentioned that you and Lexie weren't speaking at the moment. She told me to bring you to your senses.

That's a hopeless cause, though." He grinned and pointed to a tray of sandwiches. "She also brought those. Leave it to her to take care of us when she's just getting out of the hospital."

Mason shook his head. "She's a great woman."

"That she is. Got to run. See you later."

"See you." Mason waved as Dave left. Then he grabbed a sandwich and took a bite. He hadn't eaten all day. He was moping, and yeah, it had something to do with Lexie. Or everything. He missed her. A lot.

Someone knocked on the office door. Mason turned, expecting to see Dave again.

"Amber. I mean Emily." He smiled. "That'll take some getting used to. You came back."

The girl stood in his doorway, looking cleaner and more well-rested than he was used to. It was good to see her.

"You look great," he said, stepping over to give her a hug.

"Thanks. My parents dropped me off. They said they'd pick me up in an hour. I'm sure they're parked outside, though, scared that I'll run away again."

"No need to worry about that, right?" he asked, lifting his brows.

She shook her head. "You said I could continue to come here."

"And I meant that. The kids are outside. They'll be glad to see you. I'm glad, too."

"Is Ms. Lexie here?" she asked, looking around.

Everyone missed Lexie.

"Not tonight." And probably never again after the way he'd treated her. He'd overheard Clara telling Rick that Lexie had gone back to Raleigh for a job interview. That had been her plan all along, though. Carolina Shores wasn't her home. Another reason he and Lexie were never meant to be together.

"Oh." Emily frowned slightly.

"Did you see a doctor like she wanted you to?" he asked.

"This morning. Everything's fine." The teen's face lit up as she talked about the baby. "I'm almost ten weeks along. The doctor says the heartbeat is strong."

"That's great news! Lexie will be glad to hear that," he said.

"Will you tell her for me? In case I don't see her again before she leaves. She's leaving soon, right?"

Mason nodded again. "I think she is. Hopefully you'll get to see her before then, but I'll let her know."

"Tell her again that I'm really sorry for breaking into her home and eating her food."

Mason grinned. "She already forgave you for that. Lexie is one of the most generous people I know. I'm sure she was glad for you to have it."

Emily fidgeted with her hands. "Okay, well, I'm going to go say hi to the others." She turned.

"Hey, Emily?"

She looked back at him.

"Your parents weren't mad at you, were they? I told you everything would be okay."

She smiled brightly. "And you were right. I never had a reason to be afraid." She sucked in a breath. "You know what my father said when I asked him if he still loved me?"

Mason shook his head. "What?"

"Love is patient. Love is kind. It always protects, always trusts, always hopes, always perseveres." She went through all of the well-known Corinthians verse, ending with, "Love never fails." There were tears in her eyes as she finished. "He said that's what love was, and that he would always do all of these things that God spoke of because he will always love me. No matter what."

Mason nodded, feeling choked up himself.

"Bye, Mr. Mason," she said, smiling again.

"See you later, Emily." He watched her leave to visit the others, retracing the words of 1 Corinthians.

Love always trusts.

That was one area he'd had a hard time with since Kristin's accident. He seemed to be white-knuckling everything in his life instead of trusting those who'd earned it and asking for help when necessary. Lexie had earned his trust this summer, and he needed to give it to her.

If she ever set foot back in Carolina Shores.

Chapter Fifteen

The next day Lexie breathed a sigh of relief when she passed the sign welcoming passersby to Carolina Shores. Instead of going straight to her rental home, where there was only one week left on the lease, she drove to Clara and Rick's. She wanted to check on her patient and friend. Clara stepped out onto the porch as Lexie drove up, already wearing her sweatpants and sneakers.

"Going for a walk?" Lexie asked.

"Oh, yes. That's part of my prescription and I take doctor's orders very seriously. Come on, Dr. Campbell."

Lexie glanced down at her sandals. "Um, okay. Just let me just change my shoes real quick." Good thing she hadn't unpacked first. Lexie grabbed her sneakers and put them on, then stepped up beside Clara. They fell into stride together as they walked down the road. "So I'm guessing you're feeling better?"

"Worlds better." Clara nodded. "Except a little guilty about ruining things—"

Lexie held up her hand. "We're not talking about Mason on this walk. Doctor's orders." She tilted her chin to her chest and narrowed her eyes on the older woman who'd taken her in this summer.

Clara frowned. "Okay. I understand."

"Good."

"It's just been so hard for him since his wife passed away, you know?" Clara continued anyway.

Lexie's pace slowed. Mason's backstory did tug on her heartstrings. She'd been holding on to her anger and trying not to give him any excuses. That way his behavior toward her didn't hurt so badly. But the empathetic side of her, the side that cared about people and their healing, the side that had made her want to become a doctor in the first place, understood a little bit about why he'd behave in the way he did. Mason would have been relieved to know that Lexie hadn't treated Clara on her own. If he'd just let her explain that Dr. Marcus was on the case, too...

"I got sick and it scared him, dear. He's a big, strong fireman who runs toward danger. But the thought of losing someone else that he cares about terrifies him," Clara said.

Tears burned behind Lexie's eyes. "I understand that. I really do." But Mason also hadn't called. Lexie had left for two days and he hadn't appeared to miss her or regret his reaction to what'd happened between them. He may have been terrified of losing Clara, but losing Lexie didn't seem to scare him at all. That said a lot about what she meant to him.

They continued to walk around the block.

"I've been offered the job in Raleigh," Lexie told Clara as they turned a corner and headed back to the house half an hour later.

Clara gasped. "Did you take it?"

"Not yet." Lexie shook her head. "I wanted to make sure it was what I wanted first."

"Is it?" There was a worried look in Clara's eyes.

Lexie considered her answer. "I've been praying and

thinking about it. I even spoke to my grandmother about it. She told me to follow my heart. The truth is I have no idea what I'm supposed to do. What if I'm never sure? The place in Raleigh wants to know by tomorrow afternoon. And Dr. Marcus can't hold the position at the clinic forever." Her chest began to tighten as she unleashed her dilemma on Clara.

"Oh, dear. I wish I could write you a prescription and fix you up the way you did for me."

Lexie laughed. "If only it was that easy."

"Well, let me ask you—what do you *want* to do?" Clara stopped walking and studied her. Hers was a similar question to Grandma Jean's.

Mason came to mind. Lexie wanted things to be the way they were with him this summer. She wanted the future she'd begun to imagine could be hers here in Carolina Shores.

Clara nodded. "I'm guessing you already know what you want. You're just trying to talk yourself out of it. That's your head talking, dear. Like your grandmother said, your heart is where you find the answers." Clara tapped her own chest.

Lexie sucked in a deep breath. They were standing back in front of the Carlyles' house. "Thanks for the walk. And for the talk. It really helped."

Clara beamed. "Good."

"I'll come visit again soon, I promise." She stepped forward and hugged Clara. She was committed to being here for another week, but her heart wanted to stay a lot longer than that. When she'd started to imagine a future here in Carolina Shores it had started with Mason, but it'd reached past that. She'd dreamed of working with Dr. Marcus and helping him run the health care clinic. And of evening walks with Clara. Of keeping in touch with the teens at the center and watching them graduate high school and college. She'd dreamed of watching them get married one day years from now. Her dreams had taken root here, and they weren't shattered just because a piece of the puzzle had gone missing.

Lexie's heart ached at the thought of not being with Mason in her dream of the future. But she knew now, without a doubt, where she wanted to be, and that was here in Carolina Shores.

Mason walked inside the Carlyles' home a few days later after a long day at work. He'd missed dinner, but Clara was still in the kitchen. He could smell the coffee in the brewer. He was the only one who drank coffee after dark so he knew that Clara had been expecting him.

"I just wanted to check on you," he said, like he had for the past several nights.

"I'm still fine." Clara glanced over her shoulder at him. "Coffee's ready. Make yourself at home, dear."

Clara had been saying that to him since the first day he'd arrived here. And he had made himself at home. He considered this his home now, as much as anywhere he'd ever been.

He grabbed a mug from the cabinet and poured himself a serving. Then he turned and leaned against the countertop, watching as Clara rinsed the dirty dishes. "You know, I can't live here forever," he said.

Clara stopped and looked at him. She laid the dish down and dried her hands with a dishcloth. Then she stepped closer to him. "You can stay here as long as you need to. You know that. And when you're ready to move on, you'll go somewhere else." She narrowed her eyes. "But you will always have a home here, no matter where you go. And a place set at my dinner table."

Mason reached for Clara's hand and held it in his. This woman had become like a second mother to him. She'd earned his trust and, after his talk with Emily the other day, he'd been trying to do better at loving others according to 1 Corinthians. *Love always trusts.* "I really want to let go of it all," he said, suddenly feeling overwhelmed. "My fears. My worry. All these things inside me that keep me awake at night. That keep me from…" He hesitated.

Clara squeezed his hand softly. "From giving Lexie your whole heart?"

Mason met her knowing gaze. "I wasn't just talking about your house. I can't live here, in this place inside myself, forever. I'm holding on to everything so tight. It's exhausting. And I'm afraid to let someone else in because that's just one more person to hold on to." He blew out a ragged breath. "But I don't know how to let it all go," he said, hoarsely.

"Oh, Mason." Clara's eyes were shining with tears. She wrapped her arms around him and hugged him tightly. Then she pulled back and dabbed at her eyes with the end of her apron.

"Pastor Diaz told me to give my fear and worry to God." He shook his head. "I would. I will. I have. But I'm still terrified."

Clara nodded. "I know. I know it's hard." She placed her hands over his and looked at him again. "It's a daily, sometimes hourly, thing, Mason. You give your fears to God and trust Him to work things out. You do it over and over, again and again. It does get easier, I promise."

He took her words in, considering them. "I treated Lexie so bad after I took you to the hospital. You were sick and I thought you were dying. I felt helpless, like when I was holding Kristin in my arms and there was nothing I could do for her. So I reacted, and I blamed Lexie. I removed her from your care at the hospital because I thought you deserved the best." He shook his head. "Lexie is the best. She cares for people with all her heart."

"Have you apologized to her yet?"

Mason gave his head a hard shake. "Clara, I started having feelings for her this summer, and I fell in love with her," he confessed, trusting Clara with everything in his heart. "But what if—"

Clara poked a gentle finger into the middle of his chest. "Right there. Those what-ifs are God's. All of them. They're not mine and they're not yours, so stop questioning everything, Mason. What does your heart say?"

"Lexie." That's all his heart had been saying for a while now.

Clara nodded. "Apologize to her then. Trust her with your feelings. And don't let her go, Mason, because she makes you happier than I've seen you in a very long time. You'll always have your past and it will sometimes hurt, but that doesn't mean you haven't moved on with your life. You can share that pain with Lexie. You can share joy with her and hope for a wonderful future together."

Mason sucked in a breath. Then he nodded, took another breath and headed for the side door.

"Wait. That's it?" Clara had her hands on her hips when he turned around. "You know I like to be in the middle of things and know what's going on. What are you going to do?"

He smiled for the first time since arriving home from the Teen Center's camping trip. "Your advice was exactly what I needed to hear. I'm going to take it," he said.

Clara clasped her hands in front of her chest, bouncing on her heels lightly. "Oh! Go ahead then. I'll see you two for dinner tomorrow night."

Mason headed to his apartment above the garage first. He had a box of things on the top shelf of his closet that were personal to him. He reached for it and carried it to his bed, lifting the lid.

The first thing he saw was a picture of him and his late wife. He smiled, letting himself feel the ache of what had happened. Clara was right; the ache might always be there, but it didn't mean he hadn't accepted Kristin's passing. He moved the picture aside and smiled to himself as he looked at a few more treasures from his childhood. Then he lifted a navy-colored velvet box and sucked in a breath before opening the lid. His grandmother's wedding ring shined up at him. He'd kept it all these years. It wasn't the ring he'd given Kristin. She'd liked modern things, and that was okay. But Lexie valued older things that had a past and a story, like him. He didn't want to tiptoe toward her anymore. He'd always run toward things that scared him, but he wasn't scared right now. He was hopeful and excited because what Clara had said rang true in his heart. It was time to let go of his fear and worry and hold on to Lexie with everything he had, if she was willing to forgive and give him another chance.

Lexie walked her last patient of the day out of the examining room and handed her a prescription. "Come back in a few days if things don't resolve."

The young woman nodded. "Thank you so much, Lexie. I mean, Dr. Campbell."

Lexie laughed. "How about Dr. Lexie?"

"Dr. Lexie," the woman repeated.

Lexie smiled to herself as she went to go write in the

patient's chart. Dr. Marcus looked up as she took a seat beside him.

"I knew you'd be a great addition to this clinic. I'm really glad you decided to stick around."

Lexie nodded. "Me, too." She'd felt at peace about this decision since she'd made it a few days earlier. That's how she knew it was right. She started to pull off her white doctor's coat when the door to the clinic opened. It wasn't quite six o'clock yet. Patients were still welcome. "I've got this…" she started to say to Dr. Marcus. Then she saw who the patient was. Mason.

He took long, heavy strides toward the front desk. "I need to see a doctor," he said, looking serious.

Lexie turned to Dr. Marcus. "Never mind. You take this one." Because Mason didn't trust her, and he probably never would, she'd come to realize.

"Actually," Mason said, leaning against the counter. "I want *you* to check me out."

Her breath stopped. "No. I'm too inexperienced, remember? If I so much as touch someone, I might break them." She shook her head again as the pain of his treatment toward her resurfaced.

Mason turned to Dr. Marcus. "She took an oath to help the sick and hurting, right?"

Dr. Marcus nodded, folding his arms at his chest. "She did. Dr. Campbell, I think it's your professional responsibility to see this patient."

Lexie's mouth fell open. After a second, she stood. "Fine." She gestured for Mason to follow her back to one of the empty examining rooms. "Have a seat on the table," she told him, trying not to show her concern. Her gaze was traveling over him, though, looking for evidence of pain. "What's wrong?" she asked. "Did you burn yourself again?" Her gaze flicked to his hand, where she'd bandaged him a few weeks back.

"No." He continued to watch her.

"Well, why are you here?" she asked, shoving her hands in the pockets of her lab coat. "Where does it hurt?"

Slowly, he raised a hand to his chest and covered his heart. "Right here," he said.

"Your heart? Are you having chest pains? Numbness and tingling in your arm?" she asked, drawing closer and lifting her stethoscope off her chest.

"My heart hurts because of you, Lexie. Because of how I treated you."

She froze.

"Lexie, I'm sorry. I reacted badly to a situation that wasn't your fault."

She exhaled. "You're not hurt. I thought you needed a doctor, but all you need is a clear conscience." She started to pull away, but he grabbed her arm gently and stopped her. "I came here to see you because I wanted to show you that I trust you. If you want to give me a full physical, I'd let you. You're a good doctor, Lexie, and if I were having chest pains or numbness and tingling, I'd come to you. Trust is important in a relationship," he said.

Lexie swallowed the rising lump in her throat.

"I need to know, can you forgive me?" he asked, still holding her arm. He moved his hand down to hers and held it. "Please."

Releasing a breath, she stared at him for a long moment. This man had saved her life this summer. He'd been there for her when she'd needed him. He was good and kind, if not just a little overprotective. She nodded slowly. "Of course I can. It hurt when you said those things the other night, but I understand." Her gaze flicked to his hand holding hers. The simple gesture felt good. She'd missed Mason. Maybe, if nothing more, they could be friends.

He stood from the examining table, still holding on to her hand. "I trust you…and I love you, Lexie," he said, stealing her breath again. "I'm *in love* with you."

Her lips parted. There was no way she was hearing him correctly. They'd just made up and now… "What did you say?" she asked.

"I said I'm in love with you. I'm tired of pretending that I'm not. I love your gentle spirit and the way you care about everyone in your life. I love how you have fun with those kids at the Teen Center and genuinely enjoy offering your time to them. I love how you catch fish and want to throw them back. You are so giving. You're such a light in this world. You've lit up my life, that's for sure."

Lexie's eyes burned as she listened.

"I want your light back in my life. I want *you* back in my life. Forever this time."

A tear slipped down her cheek. "I love you, too, Mason," she said, as her heart burst with joy. This was the last thing she'd expected today, but her spirit was suddenly soaring. "I love how you protect the ones you love. I love how you take care of those teens and the men at the fire station. You care for Clara and Rick. And me. When I'm with you, there's nowhere else in the world I'd rather be," she told him.

Mason smiled, holding her hands a little tighter. "I was hoping you'd say that." Then he dropped to one knee in front of her.

Lexie's heart stopped beating for a second. She sucked in an audible breath.

"About that *forever* word…" He reached into his pocket and pulled out a dark blue box. Lexie trembled as he lifted the lid and presented her with a pear-shaped diamond. "It was my grandmother's ring. I thought this would be fitting since you'll be wearing your grandmother's dress. If you say yes, that is," he said, his gaze steady on hers.

Her mouth was dry. Her heart pounded. "You haven't asked me anything." Because despite how it looked, there was no way Mason was saying what she hoped he was.

"Lexie Campbell, I love you with all my broken-and-pieced-back-together heart. I want to spend my life with you. Will you marry me? Please."

Tears of joy streamed down her cheeks. She and Mason were starting on a foundation of honesty and trust. They'd worked hard this summer to build those things. They'd also fallen in love. This was a relationship that wouldn't fall apart. This time, it would last.

She held her left hand out to him and nodded. "Yes. I say yes to forever with you."

Then he slipped his grandmother's ring on her finger. "A perfect fit," he said as he rose to his feet and kissed her. Then he wrapped his arms around her, holding her tight—another perfect fit.

Epilogue

One year later

Lexie twirled in front of the mirror, wearing her grandmother's wedding dress. *Her* wedding dress. With a sideward glance, she looked at the clock. T-minus thirty minutes, and Mason hadn't bailed on her yet. Not that she ever thought he would. Not even for a second. She and Mason were committed. Their relationship was built on a foundation of love and trust. And soon they'd be man and wife.

"You look beautiful." Clara stepped inside the room and drew her hands to her mouth.

Lexie did another half twirl, laughing joyfully. "Thank you."

"I spoke to your mom and dad in the church. They're lovely people, dear. I told them I have a guest room they can stay in anytime." She winked.

"Have you seen Mason?"

Clara stepped forward and helped Lexie fasten the top buttons on the back of her dress. "He's as happy as I've ever seen him. There." She patted the last button. "I just got finished telling him this. Now it's your turn."

Lexie turned and gave Clara her full attention. "What is it?"

"Take care of Mason. He's not my real son, but I love him like he is. The same way that I love you like a daughter. Love is one of the greatest blessings. And even though you're newlyweds and are only going to want to spend time together for a while, my dinner table is always open. In fact, I'll be a little saddened by the empty chairs."

"Expect us at least once a week," Lexie said, wrapping her arms around Clara's shoulders. "Mason and I have already agreed."

"Oh. I might cry before the big event."

Lexie laughed and pulled back. "Can't have that."

"I love you both. You've added so much to mine and Rick's lives. We are so happy for you, dear."

Lexie smiled. "Thank you, Clara."

Someone knocked on the door, and Lexie sucked in a deep breath. "That's probably my father."

"I should go get seated." Clara squeezed her hand before letting go. Then she opened the door.

Lexie's father waited with a tear in his eye. "It's time," he said.

Nervous anticipation rose up inside her. All she had to do was walk down the aisle and not trip over the train of her grandmother's dress. Agreeing to spend forever with Mason was the easy part. "Okay."

Her father took her hand and held it for a long minute. "The first time I saw your mother in that dress I knew there was no one more beautiful in the world. I thought no one could ever compare. But I was wrong. You look…" He shook his head.

"Don't cry, Daddy."

"They're happy tears because my only daughter is finally happy."

Lexie nodded. She *was* happy. Her grandmother was right. God's plan for her had been better than her own.

Music began to play as she approached the aisle of the church. Standing at the entranceway, she locked eyes with Mason and took a breath, and another, suddenly feeling breathless. She glanced around the room seeing so many friends, new and old. She walked toward the front, smiling at the long line of firemen standing by her future husband. On her side was her best friend from Raleigh and several cousins. And Emily—finally safe and secure.

After kissing her cheek, her father withdrew his arm and joined her hand with Mason's.

Lexie repeated vow by vow, meaning every word.

"I do," she said.

"I do," he said.

Then, in the span of what felt like a heartbeat, it was over. She and Mason shared their first kiss as husband and wife while the crowd cheered. But all Lexie could see was Mason. They exited the church and dipped into his truck outside, finally alone.

"I'm glad you turned down the limo," she said. "This is much more us."

"Can't hardly go camping in a limo, can we?"

She shook her head, grinning. They'd both agreed that going on the Teen Center's second annual camping trip tomorrow was as good a way as any to start their marriage. Followed by a romantic week in Charleston, South Carolina.

Lexie gave Mason a serious look. "Do you vow to scare away all the bears and snakes, and every other creepy critter for as long as we both shall camp?"

"I do." He leaned in to kiss her. "And toss back all the fish we catch together, too."

Lexie giggled, happy to have a second alone with him. "And promise to love me when I burn dinner?"

He took her hand. "I thought we went over this already. I will love you forever, no matter what, through sickness and health." His eyes softened, and Lexie knew his memories of Kristin were surfacing. She didn't mind. She knew it didn't lessen his love for her.

"For as long as we both shall live," she said, repeating the vows they'd just made to one another in the church.

He nodded, his eyes glazed with tears. Hers were, too. He leaned in and kissed her softly, and then cranked the truck's engine. The fleet of fire trucks ahead of them turned on their lights. "Here we go, Mrs. Benfield."

"I like the sound of that."

He winked and followed the fire trucks. "Me, too. I figure giving you my last name is the least I can do."

"For what?" she asked.

"For breaking through those evacuation barriers last summer, and giving me a second chance at love."

Lexie's heart swelled with an indescribable joy. It was a second chance at love for both of them. And the last chance. Because this love would last forever.

* * * * *

If you liked this book, try these other Love Inspired stories filled with emotional moments:

THE DAD NEXT DOOR by Stephanie Dees
HOMETOWN HERO'S REDEMPTION
by Jill Kemerer
THE SOLDIER'S SECRET CHILD
by Lee Tobin McClain
THE BACHELOR'S UNEXPECTED FAMILY
by Lisa Carter

Available now from Love Inspired!

Find more great reads at www.LoveInspired.com

Dear Reader,

When making plans for our future, we should remember to do so with a healthy dose of prayer and seeking God's guidance. His plans for our lives are always better than the ones we create for ourselves.

Lexie had her life all planned out. She was going to marry and start a new job as a doctor in the city. Those plans fell through, though, and led her to Carolina Shores and work at one of the last places she thought she'd end up. It also led her to Mason and exactly where God needed her to be.

After losing his first wife, Mason thought he would remain alone forever. That might be what God has in His plans for other widowers, but it wasn't what He had in store for Mason. Once Mason aligned himself with God's master plan, he was blessed with a new relationship and hope for the future.

I hope you enjoyed reading *Healing His Widowed Heart!* I welcome comments and letters at anniehemby@gmail.com.

God Bless,
Annie

COMING NEXT MONTH FROM
Love Inspired®

Available September 19, 2017

AMISH CHRISTMAS TWINS
Christmas Twins • by Patricia Davids

After returning to her Amish community, pregnant widow and mom of twins Willa Chase is devastated when her grandfather turns her away. An accident strands her at the home of John Miller—jolting the reclusive widower out of sorrow and into a Christmas full of joy and hope for a second chance at family.

THE RANCHER'S MISTLETOE BRIDE
Wyoming Cowboys • by Jill Kemerer

Managing Lexi Harrington's newly inherited ranch through the holidays might not have been cowboy Clint Romine's brightest idea. Getting close to her means revealing secrets he's long kept hidden. And falling for her means he'll have to have to convince Lexi her home isn't back in the big city—but in his arms.

AN ALASKAN CHRISTMAS
Alaskan Grooms • by Belle Calhoune

Single mom Maggie Richards is ready to embrace a new future in Love, Alaska—restoring the gift shop she's inherited in time for Christmas. But she gets a blast from the past when childhood pal Finn O'Rourke offers help. With both of them working together, will love become the most unexpected holiday gift of all?

MOUNTAIN COUNTRY COWBOY
Hearts of Hunter Ridge • by Glynna Kaye

For cowboy Cash Herrera, taking a job at Hunter's Hideaway ranch is a chance to gain custody of his son—and work for lovely Rio Hunter. Rio knows the secret she's keeping means leaving Hunter Ridge, but spending time with Cash and his little boy has her wishing for a home with the man who's claiming her heart.

MENDING THE WIDOW'S HEART
Liberty Creek • by Mia Ross

From her first meeting with Sam Calhoun, military widow and single mom Holly Andrews feels a surprising kinship. But she's not looking for permanence. Working on a youth baseball league together rekindles dreams Sam had all but abandoned. Can he convince Holly to stay in Liberty Creek, with him, forever?

A BABY FOR THE DOCTOR
Family Blessings • by Stephanie Dees

Jordan Conley knows Dr. Ash Sheehan would be a perfect pediatrician for her new foster son—but her heart-pounding crush on the confirmed bachelor complicates things. Besides, she's horses and hay, and he's fancy suits. But the more involved he gets in their lives, the more she wishes they could stay together...always.

Get 2 Free Books,
Plus 2 Free Gifts—
just for trying the Reader Service!

Love Inspired®

LI17R2

John waited beside Samuel's sleigh and tried
unsuccessfully to curb his excitement. He was almost as
giddy as Megan and Lucy. A sleigh ride with Willa at his
side was his idea of the perfect winter evening, especially
since he didn't have to drive. Lucy was the first one out of
the house. She quickly claimed her spot in the front seat
beside Samuel. Megan came out next and scrambled up
beside her sister. He'd never seen the twins so delighted.

Willa took John's hand as he helped her in. He gave
her gloved fingers a quick squeeze and saw her smile
before she looked down.

Samuel slapped the lines and the big horse took off
down the snow-covered lane. Sleigh bells jingled merrily
in time with the horse's footfalls, and Megan and Lucy
tried to catch snowflakes on their tongues between
giggles.

John leaned down to see Willa's face. "Are you warm

enough?" She nodded, but her cheeks looked rosy and cold. John took off his woolen scarf and wrapped it around her head to cover her mouth and nose.

"*Danki,*" she murmured.

"Don't mention it. In spite of the cold, it's a lovely evening to go caroling, isn't it?" The thick snow obscured the horizon and made it feel as if they were riding inside a glass snow globe. The fields lay hidden under a thick blanket of white. A hushed stillness filled the air, broken only by the jingle of the harness bells and the muffled thudding of the horse's feet.

Their first destination was only a mile from John's house. As Lucy and Megan scrambled down from the sleigh, John offered Willa his hand to help her out.

"Was this what you imagined Christmas would be like when you decided to return to your Amish family?"

She shook her head. "I never imagined anything like this. Do you do it every year?"

"We do."

"You aren't going to actually sing, are you, John?"

He threw back his head and laughed. "*Nee,* but I will hum along."

"Softly, dear, softly," she suggested.

He wondered if she realized that she had called him "dear." It was turning out to be an even more wonderful night than he had hoped for.

Don't miss
AMISH CHRISTMAS TWINS
by Patricia Davids, available October 2017 wherever
Love Inspired® books and ebooks are sold.

www.LoveInspired.com

SPECIAL EXCERPT FROM

Love Inspired HISTORICAL

*When Annie Marshall answers single father
Hugh Arness's ad for a marriage in name only, the
preacher refuses—she's too young and pretty to be
happy in a loveless union. But after he agrees to Annie's
suggestion of a four-week trial period, Hugh might just
realize they're the perfect match.*

Read on for a sneak preview of
MONTANA BRIDE BY CHRISTMAS by **Linda Ford**,
available October 2017 from Love Inspired Historical!

"Mr. Arness—I'm sorry, Preacher Arness—I'm here to
apply for this position."

"How old are you, Miss Marshall?"

"I'm nineteen, but I've been looking after my brothers,
my father, my grandfather and, until recently, my niece
since I was fourteen. I think I can manage to look after
one four-year-old boy."

That might be so, and he would have agreed in any
other case but this four-year-old was his son, Evan, and
Annie Marshall simply did not suit. She was too young.
Too idealistic. Too fond of fun.

She flipped the paper back and forth, her eyes narrowed
as if she meant to call him to task.

"Are you going back on your word?" she insisted,
edging closer.

"I've not given my word to anything."

"'Widower with four-year-old son seeking a marriage of convenience. Prefer someone older with no expectations of romance. I'm kind and trustworthy. My son needs lots of patience and affection. Interested parties please see Preacher Arness at the church.' I'm applying," Annie said with conviction and challenge.

"You're too young and…" He couldn't think how to voice his objections without sounding unkind, and having just stated the opposite in his little ad, he chose to say nothing.

"Are you saying I'm unsuitable?" She spoke with all the authority one might expect from a Marshall…but not from a woman trying to convince him to let her take care of his son.

He met her challenging look with calm indifference. Unless she meant to call on her three brothers and her father and grandfather to support her cause, he had nothing to fear from her. He needed someone less likely to chase after excitement and adventure. She'd certainly find none here as the preacher's wife.

"I would never say such a thing, but like the ad says, Evan needs a mature woman." And he'd settle for a plain one, and especially a docile one.

"From what I hear, he needs someone who understands his fears." She leaned back as if that settled it.

Copyright © 2017 by Linda Ford

LIHEXP0917